Richard Carpenter's

ROBIN OF SHERWOOD

THE WATERFORD BOY

Richard Carpenter's Robin of Sherwood
The Waterford Boy
By Jennifer Ash
First published in 2021
This revised edition
Published in 2025 by
Chinbeard Books

in association with
Oak Tree Books
oaktreebooks.uk

Editor: Barnaby Eaton-Jones
Sub Editor: Harriet Whitehouse

Richard Carpenter's

ROBIN OF SHERWOOD

THE WATERFORD BOY

by
Jennifer Ash

A Chinbeard Books / Oak Tree Books Original

PROLOGUE

It was raining. Not a cold, wet downpour but a fine reviving spray being carried on the soothing breeze. It waltzed through the leaves of Sherwood Forest, stirring the trees into finally letting go of the last foothold of a harsh winter and welcoming the touch of spring.

In the village of Waterford, nestled on the north edge of Sherwood, the gentle rustle of leaves was accompanied by the persistent trickle of water which wound its way through the shallow ford that gave the village its name.

Sat in a small building—more a hut than a cottage—at the very edge of the small settlement, Alwin of Waterford's jaws worked hard against the crust of bread his mother, Dora, had thrust at him for breakfast. He watched as she poked at the fire, the room's main source of heat and light.

'We need more firewood, Alwin. Will you—'

'Yes, Mother.' Not waiting until he'd finished his last mouthful, he grabbed Dora's work-roughened hand, dragging her across the small square of garden that divided their home from the edge of the forest.

'Alwin! I have my chores to do.'

'It won't take long.'

Hooking her skirt and apron up in one hand as her son dragged her past their vegetable patch towards the edge of Sherwood, Dora failed to keep the exasperation from her voice. 'You don't need to do this ritual anymore, Alwin.'

'Of course I do. I *must*. My ritual keeps us safe.' Speaking with a certainty that unnerved Dora, Alwin brought them to a halt beneath the oak tree that stood nearest the forest.

Tilting his small round face up at its branches, Alwin freed his mother's hand before pushing his shock of brown hair from his eyes. Silent for a moment, he observed the sway of the tree—a tree he'd always thought of as his own. Ribbons were tied to the branches, and pebbles and loose twigs had been reverently placed upon the thicker lower branches—offerings to Herne the Hunter, Lord of the Trees.

Peering anxiously over her shoulder, Dora watched as the ribbons fluttered in the breeze, their bright colours gleaming in the early morning light. 'But son, people are talking.'

'It's important.' Alwin suddenly sounded like a tiny toddler who was about to stamp his feet in temper, rather than a young man of twelve.

Dora swallowed back a sigh. Since the death of her husband two years ago, Alwin had been the man of the house. Sometimes she forgot he was bearing so much responsibility for one so young. It was only natural he'd want to hold onto a habit developed out of grief for a father he'd adored. 'They'll be trouble soon, Alwin. All I asked you to do was fetch some wood from the forest. It's but a moment's work.'

'But I have to do this before I go into the forest. I *have* to, Mother.'

Weak in the face of her son's unshakeable determination, Dora placed a hand on his shoulder. 'I'm afraid. I don't want to lose you too.'

As if answering Dora's concerns for her son's safety, the wind picked up and whistled through the branches above them. Somehow the gust missed all the other trees in the forest, as if the ribboned tree alone was clapping its leaves at Alwin in encouragement.

'This tree looks after us, Mother. It always has.' He patted the trunk affectionately. 'It always will.'

'I could understand it if you were off to war, or even embarking on a trip into Nottingham or up to Newark, but you're only going into Sherwood to fetch firewood.'

'You don't understand, Mother.'

'I understand that the villagers are whispering witchcraft.'

Alwin took one of his mother's palms and pressed it lightly against the tree's trunk. 'They are wrong.'

Making one final plea to her son as the unseasonal warmth of the bark surprised her, Dora said, 'But son, Herne will protect us anyway.'

Alwin's big brown eyes met his mother's. They reflected far more pain back at her than any twelve -year old's eyes should bear. 'You don't want me disappearing when I'm in Sherwood like Father did, do you?'

Fear crept up Dora's spine. 'Your father was killed by evil soldiers carrying out evil orders. He was not killed by the forest itself.'

'I don't want to take the chance. Anyway,' Alwin's habitual smile was already back in place as he returned his gaze to the tree, 'it won't take long. Please, Mother. It helps. I know it does.' He patted the bark with affection.

'Well, this has to be last time. The very last time.'

Lifting her son off the ground, saddened by how skinny his once robust frame had become since she'd had no husband to provide for them, Dora helped lever Alwin into the bottom branches. As he climbed, she took another glance over her shoulder in case any of the other early risers in the village were watching.

'Can you pass me a twig from the ground please, Mother? I forgot to collect one before I climbed up.'

Wishing he'd hurry, Dora scrabbled through the pile of twigs Alwin kept at the base of the tree. 'Here. Quickly!'

'Thank you.'

Sat with his feet dangling off the branch, Alwin's genial expression became serious as he tapped the twig three times against the trunk.

Dora shivered as she saw her son's eyes closing. She'd seen him perform this ceremony so many times, yet it still filled her with as much wonder as it did apprehension as the air around her son froze. She always had the feeling that the earth itself was listening to her boy sing his words to the forest.

Sometimes she was convinced that the calm the trees commanded was only ever seconds away from screaming.

'Mighty forest, I beseech thee, through the strength of this ritual, and the power of Herne, Lord of the Trees; protect my mother and all who live under the shadow of Sherwood.'

The moment the words were spoken, Alwin opened his eyes and his countenance returned to a happy calm. Without hesitating, he jumped to the ground. As his body left the branch, the delicate breeze took up from where it had left off, as if it had merely been catching its breath.

Engulfing his mother, Alwin gave her a huge hug.

Muffled by her son's arms, Dora couldn't help but laugh. 'Your embraces are all awkward, just like your father's were.'

'I'll always care for you, Mother. I want to make Father proud.'

'He was always proud of you, Alwin. I'm sure he still is.'

Alwin sounded wistful, 'You think so?'

'I know so. Now then, you've done your ritual, so get that firewood collected. Don't be long, there's work to be done.'

Watching her son run into the forest, Dora patted the ritual tree. 'Herne, please, protect my boy.'

Two horses waited restlessly under the cover of the narrow band of trees that divided the edge of the forest and the village of Waterford. Their hooves stamped, keen to be on their way, as their riders covertly observed the activity in the garden of the nearby cottage.

'Should I chase the boy, my Lord Gisburne?' The captain of the guard sneered out his words, fully expecting he'd be commanded to give chase.

Sir Guy of Gisburne gave a snort. 'If the Sheriff of Nottingham hadn't ordered us back to Nottingham to greet a guest, I'd have already commanded it.'

'But we heard him utter blasphemy to a false god, my Lord?'

Never in the mood to be questioned by his ambitious subordinate, Gisburne snapped back, 'I won't forget what we've seen and heard, Captain. Come.'

'My Lord.'

'Come!' Gisburne urged his horse forward with a sharp kick, 'We will return. I can promise you that.'

CHAPTER ONE

The fire in the great hall of Nottingham castle had diminished to a mere flicker, but Robert de Rainault, High Sheriff of Nottingham, was too flushed with anger to be anything other than hot.

Servants moved with wary caution, almost on tiptoes, as they cleared away dirty platters and served fresh food to the seated sheriff. No one wanted to make a mistake and accidentally become the final spark that lit the fuse on his notoriously short temper. The sheriff, however, hardly noticed his long-suffering staff. He was too busy fuming as he listened to the fast-retreating footfall of the King's clerk, who'd just run from his presence.

The sheriff gave a humourless grin as he slumped back in his chair. 'I bet that wretch is already worrying about how to deliver my reply to his master's message without getting flayed for his trouble.'

Seconds later, a new set of footsteps could be heard and Sir Guy of Gisburne strode into the hall. A glance at the sheriff's brooding expression made him groan as he passed deeper into the vast stone room; the chill within was a sharp contrast to the heat of the saddle. He grabbed a servant by the shoulder. 'See to the fire, woman. What are you thinking, letting it get so low?'

Not waiting to hear her blustering apology, the sheriff's steward continued to where De Rainault sat, on a raised dais, to the very back of the hall.

'You're late, Gisburne.'

'My horse went lame. I had to swap mounts with the captain.'

'My heart bleeds.' The sheriff stabbed a piece of meat with the point of his knife. 'And so, the captain of the guard would now be leading a lame horse all the way to Nottingham on foot?'

'The exercise will do him good.'

The sheriff snorted, gripping his dagger tighter. 'You should have heard him, Gisburne!'

'The captain, my Lord?'

'No, you dolt. The clerk from the King. The man you were *supposed* to be here to greet with me.'

'The man I saw fleeing from the castle, my Lord?'

Not replying to Gisburne's question, De Rainault stared into the reignited flames of the hall fire. 'It has to be a joke. *Fifty* men. It's ridiculous.'

With exaggerated patience Gisburne asked, '*What* has to be a joke, my Lord Sheriff?'

'*If* you'd have been here on time as I instructed, you'd know that our beloved King John wants me to provide more men to fight in his cursed French war. Fifty of them.'

'Fifty men, my Lord?'

'I trust you can count that high?'

Gisburne hid his response to the sheriff's jibe by scrapping the legs of a wooden seat hard against the flagstone floor as he pulled it out from beneath the table. Sitting down, Guy signalled to the nearest servant to bring him a drink. He had a feeling he was going to need one as the sheriff went on.

'And I'm not in a position to argue. Look at this.' With an air of disgust, the sheriff flapped a rolled-out parchment in his steward's direction.

Snatching it from De Rainault's fingers, Gisburne began to read. 'This says we're to empty the prisons, my Lord. Nothing unusual in that.'

'True, but our prisoners are often so long awaiting the court that they barely have the strength

3

to stand, let alone fight.' Wrapping his bejewelled fingers around a goblet, the sheriff drank quickly, before crashing the cup back against the table. 'It's ridiculous, Gisburne! If King John wants men to fight for him then he should send his own soldiers to collect them, not leave it to us to scoop them up from the four corners of the county.'

'Perhaps the king requires more troops because the French war is proving expensive in manpower, my Lord.'

'You mean the country's men folk are being slaughtered wholesale.' Taking another noisy mouthful of wine, the sheriff added, 'And now John's run out of willing volunteers to fight, he's scraping around for bodies that have no choice in the matter. And do you know what that insufferable clerk said when I pointed that fact out?'

Well used to his master's petulance, his voice brittle, Gisburne said, 'I dread to think, my Lord.'

'He said, Gisburne, that no one has a choice if the king bids them do something.'

'He *is* the king, my Lord.'

'Don't you start, Gisburne.'

Scowling as he re-read the parchment, Sir Guy ventured, 'But surely, my Lord, if you don't send men to fetch the prisoners from Nottinghamshire's gaols, including Newark's, then the king will not be happy.'

'The king is never happy. He was probably dropped on his head when he was a child.'

Gisburne laughed without humour as a servant brought him plate of meat and a fresh jug of wine for the table. 'Newark Castle is miles away. When are we to have these prisoners ready for collection, my Lord?'

'If you'd bothered to read to the very end of the document you're holding, you'd know that King John has assigned his chief recruiter, Sir James D'Marelle, to carry out this dubious task. He is currently on a circuit of England.'

The stiff parchment gave a creak as Gisburne's forefinger and thumb squeezed it tighter. His eyes darted to the very bottom of the document, already knowing it was pointless to hope the sheriff had been wrong about the identity of the man on his way to the castle. 'D'Marelle...' His words trailed off, but his thoughts rang clear. *Not him. Not here.*

Oblivious to his steward's discomfort, the sheriff went on. 'According to that cowardly clerk, D'Marelle will be arriving here, in Nottingham, in just a day or two; expecting to take our contribution to the Lincolnshire coast.'

'James D'Marelle is not a man to argue with, my Lord.' Gisburne's unsettled countenance betrayed him, and for the first time the sheriff was aware that his steward wasn't being his usual surly self.

'You've met him, Gisburne?'

'Unfortunately.' Gisburne opened his mouth to explain, but his master had already lost interest and had returned, instead, to the matter in hand.

'The clerk was keen to stress that James D'Marelle is not a man to be taken lightly. If we don't have the stated number of men ready when he gets here, then he'll stay in the castle until he has what the king demands.'

'How inconvenient for you, my Lord.' Sir Guy didn't bother to hide how little he cared. As long as he could stay as far away from D'Marelle as possible, whatever the sheriff had to put up with was not his problem.

'Not as inconvenient as the fine the king will impose on Nottingham if we fail him.'

Gisburne asked more out of duty than interest, 'Fine, my Lord?'

'The cost of paying for fifty mercenaries to be sent to France instead—if we can't produce enough prisoners.'

'Inconvenient *and* expensive, my Lord.'

The sharp retort rising in De Rainault's throat was forgotten at the sound of unfamiliar footsteps approaching. They told of sturdy leather boots, which cared not if they walked in the halls of king's or the villages of peasants.

'Who the hell is here now?' The sheriff flapped a hand towards the steps at the corner of the hall where he could see the castle steward talking to a stranger. 'Go and find out, Gisburne.'

From his throne-like chair behind the hall's high table, the sheriff's hawk-like eyes never left the activity at the edge of the room. He observed the scene shrewdly, as the owner of the sturdy sounding boots and his deputy exchanged some hastily muttered words, before a grim-faced Gisburne returned to his side.

'Well, Gisburne?'

'That was a messenger, direct from James D'Marelle, my Lord. The recruiter will be here tomorrow.'

'Tomorrow!' Jumping to his feet, the sheriff slammed his goblet against the hefty oak table. 'How are we supposed to have fifty men ready by tomorrow?'

Guy didn't bother to sit down again. 'Do you want me to leave for Newark castle now, my Lord?'

'No, I don't. Sit down, Gisburne. I told you, you're not going that far.' His livid expression morphed into one of pure cunning. 'We need to think.'

Gisburne sat as instructed, risking the sheriff's ire by saying, 'But, my Lord, if D'Marelle…'

De Rainault wasn't listening. 'The King's clerk was a miserable little man, Gisburne, but he did make one good point. If John wants fifty men, he will have to have fifty men.'

The evil smirk that spread across his master's face was contagious, and a grinning Gisburne automatically shuffled his chair a little closer to hear his latest conspiracy. 'You're planning something, my Lord?'

'In a manner of speaking, Gisburne. In a manner of speaking.' The sheriff lowered his voice, so they weren't overheard. 'Now listen carefully. You will empty the gaol here, in the castle, and the other nearby gaols, but as for the rest… We'll impose a tax. A people tax. The Crown has always had a fondness for taxes after all.' The sheriff snatched the parchment off the table as he spoke and waved it in his fist. 'These orders are fairly clear, but it wouldn't take much to interpret the king's wishes in our own way. I want you to make a collection of local men. I'm sure you can use your imagination.'

'An excellent suggestion, my Lord. Umm...
What sort of local men exactly?'

Rolling his eyes De Rainault bit back the urge
to shout, 'Oh, for goodness sake, Gisburne. Do I
have to think of everything for you? The idle, the
beggars, the thieves, the mad, and most of all, the
troublemakers that plague this county. Anyone,
Gisburne. As long as they are male and can hold a
sword!'

CHAPTER TWO

The soldiers rode hard and fast from the gates of Nottingham Castle, while escorting a horse pulling a cart; empty, and ready to be filled with unsuspecting men.

The winding road that skirted Sherwood was no place for soldiers to linger. Robin Hood and his followers had been established in the forest long enough for any man working for a figure of ambitious authority to be wary of the possibility of an outlaw's arrow in their back. Sir Guy of Gisburne was more aware than most of the cost of the county's most revered outlaws residing so close to Nottingham. His pride had been dented by Robin Hood and his men, interfering with matters that didn't concern them, on more occasions than he cared to recall.

After an hour's ride, they drew close to Gisburne's intended destination. Lifting his right hand to signal his men to slow to a walk, he winced as the empty cart bumped and skittered across the dirt-covered road,

Hoping the sound hadn't alerted the residents of the village ahead to the danger that approached, Sir Guy seized hold of his sword as the captain of the guard turned to him, a satisfied expression on his face.

'We approach Waterford, my Lord.'

'The king has given us the perfect opportunity to rid the shire of the work-shy and the useless, Captain. Let's make the most of it. We'll start here.'

The captain's lips twisted into a cruel smile. 'The pagan boy, my Lord?'

'Precisely.'

Alwin hummed happily as he tied a new ribbon into the branches of his ritual tree. Admiring the strip of pale blue material, he picked up a slim twig and closed his eyes. The crisp morning air caressed his round cheeks as he drummed the stick against

the trunk. He'd only got halfway through the first line of his chant when a trickle of unease ran up his spine. Pausing, Alwin slowly opened his eyes.

The faint sound, that he'd felt rather than heard, remained. The steady pad of approaching hooves. Motionless, hardly daring to breath, Alwin strained his ears to listen.

There were at least three horses, maybe more. This was not a lone merchant who'd lost his way and was hoping for refreshment and the chance to sell his wares across a kitchen table.

Shifting his position cautiously, Alwin tucked his legs up onto the branch and rocked onto his knees. Holding the trunk to balance him, he tried to get a view of what, so far, he'd only heard. The hairs on the back of his neck vibrated. Every fibre in his being told him that danger was very near.

The gasp that escaped Alwin's lips, when he saw the source of the sound, made him clamp a hand to his mouth—afraid that even his thoughts might be overheard.

Sir Guy of Gisburne and at least three soldiers were sat on horses. Unmoving, they lurked behind a thin band of trees that separated his home, and the ford, from the road which ran from to Nottingham and Newark.

Mutely uttering up a private plea to Herne for the men to move on and leave Waterford in peace, Alwin clutched his twig tighter. Edging closer to the trunk, determined not to make a sound, he was equally determined to finish his ritual. Whatever the Sheriff of Nottingham's steward wanted, Alwin was sure that it would not be good, and that Waterford would need the protection his ritual afforded more than ever.

Tapping the trunk again, not allowing the contact of wood on wood to make a noise, Alwin thought about the rumours that followed the brash Norman soldier the villagers referred to as Guy the Gamekeeper. The name had been earned by Gisburne's brutal and uncompromising treatment of anyone caught poaching in the forest—or of anyone who was caught in the forest without a good explanation, come to that.

Like Father.

A frisson of terror ran through Alwin. Keeping his eyes fixed upon the glimpse of Gisburne's blonde hair that glinted through the trees in the early morning sunshine, Alwin resumed his chant within the safety of his own head. *Mighty forest, I beseech thee, through the power of this ritual, and the strength of...*

Suddenly, one of the horses whinnied, shattering the silence, making Alwin jump and dropping his stick to the ground as his nerves kicked in.

'My Lord!'

The imperial tones of Gisburne's captain of the guard rang out and panic gripped Alwin. Chanting faster, he huddled against the trunk as the horses got closer.

Gisburne's response echoed across the garden. 'If the king wants men to fight in France, Captain, then we'd better make a start collecting some.'

'My pleasure, my Lord.'

The sound of twigs breaking beneath hooves was lost beneath the bellow of Gisburne's terrifying order. 'Make your men ready to fetch the Waterford boy.'

The Waterford boy? He can't mean me?

Remembering his mother's warning about his ritual frightening people, Alwin apologised to Herne as he jumped from the tree. Then, unsure what to do next, the boy stood, frozen to the spot.

Should he run? If he did, which way should he go? Towards his mother to warn her, or into the forest to safety?

Gisburne took the decision from his shoulders.

'The heathen boy! There!' His sharp shout rang in Alwin's ears. 'He's going to escape. Grab him.'

14

In less than a second, two soldiers were running across the ford on foot.

Shouting for help with each step, Alwin ran as fast as he could towards Sherwood. The pounding of his feet was only eclipsed by the hammering of the soldier's solid boots as they maintained their pursuit.

Alwin's ears continued to strain for any sound; any noise which might signify that help was coming. But all he could hear was the shout of the captain.

'Idiots! Grab him before he escapes into the forest.'

'No!' Alwin stumbled over a tree root as he reached the edge of Sherwood. He was sure he could feel the soldier's breath on the back of his neck.

Alwin had no idea where he was going, he just knew he had to keep moving. Fear leant his legs strength. As he fled, Alwin spoke to Herne. He knew the sound of him speaking his ritual would make it easier for the soldiers to track him, but it also gave him the nerve to keep running into the unknown.

'Herne, keep me safe. Mother! Keep her safe. Please...' His voice snagged in his throat as he fled, his words coming out faster and faster, tumbling out in muddled whisper. 'Herne, Lord of the trees... protect my—'

Abruptly, the light breeze whipped up into a stronger wind, shaking the leaves like rattles, pushing the soldiers back, slowing them as they chased their quarry through the trees.

Unaware of the change in the air just behind him, missing the curses of the soldiers labouring against a whirlwind that had sprung from nowhere, Alwin kept going.

'I'm so sorry I didn't finish my ritual… I can't…' His words were little more than gasps now, and he knew he'd have to stop soon. The desire to drop to the floor was becoming overwhelming. 'Herne… the ritual… not finished… Which way? Which way do I go?'

Half running, half limping, into an area of thicket trees, Alwin clasped his hands to his aching sides; slowing down despite himself. The forest around him grew denser and darker, and suddenly Alwin realised he couldn't hear any footsteps but his own.

Hardly daring to believe he'd outrun his pursuers, he hobbled onwards, but still no soldiers loomed up behind him. No rough hands reached out to haul him towards the castle prison for a crime he hadn't know he'd committed. Alwin could hear nothing, except for the faint and reassuring hum of the leaves dancing in the trees above.

Gisburne's face shone red with anger. He didn't shout, but each word he uttered was bitten off and spat out at the soldiers as they returned to Waterford.

'You… let… him… escape.'

'My Lord, we—' The first of the two men-at-arms had his explanation cut short by the slap of a mailed hand across his face.

'You fools.'

Alwin didn't allow himself to stay where he was for long. He might not be able to see or hear the soldiers, but that didn't mean they weren't nearby.

Allowing himself just enough time to take a few deep gasps off fresh forest air, he began to move forward again, blindly pushing his way through the trees, his direction aimless, his thinly soled boots snapping and cracking leaves and fallen wood beneath his stumbling tread.

Continuing to talk to himself as he went, Alwin

puffed out his words. 'I didn't finish my chant before I came into Sherwood. What will happen? Something bad... Something bad is going to happen, I just know it is. Herne, help me please... I'm sorry. Herne, I'm sorry I...'

CHAPTER THREE

Much pulled the string back on his bow. The deer wasn't the biggest he'd ever seen, but it was large enough to provide the outlaws with enough meat for the next few days.

The youngest of Robin Hood's outlaw band steadied his aim. His firm fingers flexed against the bowstring, but as he prepared to let the arrow fly, a light humming caught his ears. Lowering his bow with a curse, Much stepped back into the cover of the trees.

The deer's ears pricked, and in seconds it was gone; swallowed up in the depths of Sherwood. Much gave a muted moan of loss. His mouth had been getting ready to taste venison, and now it looked as though they'd be eating yet more of the fish Little John was so fond of catching for dinner.

Remaining motionless, Much heard the sound that had disturbed his hunt again. Clumsily careless footsteps were weaving through the forest. They were too haphazard to belong to a soldier, and too irregular to be a poacher. A few seconds later, the outlaw saw the lithe figure of a young man passing through Sherwood.

Not moving from his hiding place, Much called out, 'Who's there?'

Oblivious to the presence of Much, Alwin blundered on, his head full of nothing but his own troubles, 'Herne, I don't want to go to France. What would my mother do without me?'

Stepping out in front of the boy, Much kept his arrow notched to his bow, but he didn't point it at the stranger. 'Who are you?'

Yelping in horror, Alwin took three hasty steps backwards and fell over a fallen branch. 'Don't hurt me.'

Seeing that the lad was younger than he first appeared to be, and clearly terrified, Much relaxed the hold of his bow and un-notched the arrow. 'I won't hurt you. What are you doing here?'

'Running.'

'I can see that! Who are you?' Much peered into the area of forest the boy had just crashed through, 'Are you on your own?'

'I'm Alwin. Alwin of Waterford. I'm always on my own. Apart from my mother.'

'What are you running from?'

'My Lord of Gisburne.'

Instantly on his guard, Much grabbed Alwin's shoulder, getting them both under cover as fast as possible; his bow back in hands. 'Gisburne? Where?'

Alarmed by how fast Much had mobilised at the mention of the sheriff's deputy, Alwin stuttered, 'In Waterford.'

'That's two miles away.' Sighing with relief, Much lowered his bow again and removed the arrow with a quiet click. 'Why did you say he was here?'

Alwin's forehead creased in confusion, 'I didn't.'

'But you... Never mind. Why were you calling for Herne?' Now the threat of danger had passed, Much began to relax. 'You do know he's probably busy doing important magical stuff.'

Agitated, Alwin shook his head. 'I never finished my ritual. And then the soldiers came. I had to run. I don't want to go to France.'

Confused, Much frowned, 'Nor do I. Why are you going to France?'

'I'm not, I'm going to hide. But I didn't do my ritual.'

Finding it hard to keep track, Much asked, 'Umm, what ritual?'

Alwin was becoming more nervous and fidgety. He kept glancing over his shoulder as if he expected to see Gisburne crash through the trees behind them.

'Can't you keep still, Alwin? You're making so much noise, someone might hear us.'

Alwin froze like a statute, his eyes wide with dismay. 'I promised Mother I'd look after her. But France is so far away!'

Putting a comforting hand on Alwin's shoulder, Much said, 'I think we'd better talk to Robin.'

'Robin?'

Much's chest puffed out proudly. 'Robin Hood. He's my friend.'

'Herne's Son is your friend?' Alwin opened his mouth in wonder.

'Yes, he is. This way.' Much pointed along a slim pathway to the left, 'He'll know what to do. Robin always knows what to do.'

CHAPTER FOUR

The flames of the campfire crackled and popped in accompaniment to the birds singing overheard. Friar Tuck stirred a wooden spoon through the contents of a large cooking pot. Grinning as he inhaled the delicious aroma's coming from the meal he was preparing, he let the good-natured bickering of his fellow outlaws wash over him.

Will Scarlet waved the arrow in his hand to emphasise the point he was making. 'And I'm telling you John, that the best place to get new arrows is Papplewick.'

Little John shook his head, 'No, lad; Wickham. Wickham's always been the best.'

Conceding somewhat, Will said, 'Wickham *was* the best, but now it's Papplewick. No question.'

Listening with good humour, Robin rested back against a tree, and pushed his blonde hair out of his eyes, before he joined the debate. 'They're both good for arrows. Any chance of that food today, Tuck?'

Ripping up a handful of herbs and throwing them into the pot with a satisfying splash, Tuck resumed his stirring; the spoon knocking against the cauldron's metal sides with happy abandon. 'Patience, Robin. I can only cook so fast.'

'Or so slowly.' Nasir added.

Tuck rolled his eyes. Every day it was the same. There was nothing worse than a hungry outlaw. 'Alright Nasir, breakfast is coming.'

As if on cue, Little John's stomach gave a loud rumble that sent Will's hand automatically reaching for his dagger in alarm. He withdrew it with a tut.

Marion laughed, 'Heavens John, didn't you eat yesterday?'

'Not enough, lass.'

Pretending to poke his friend with his dagger, Will said, 'It takes a hell of a lot to fill John's long legs, Marion.'

'Alright, alright, I'm just hungry that's—' A faint sound cut through the clearing. John leapt to his feet, scooping his knife up as he did so. 'Someone's coming.' He hissed.

The outlaws barely drew breath as Nasir held up two fingers to signal that there were two sets of feet approaching.

Tuck and John reached for their staves, holding them close, as Robin and Marion drew their bows, and Will placed his hand on the hilt of his ever-ready sword.

'It's Much!' John relaxed his squared shoulders and lowered his staff. 'You could have got yourself killed, blundering towards the camp like that.'

Giving the men a stern look, which told them not to give Much a hard time, Marion asked, 'Who's your friend, Much?'

'This is Alwin. I found him.'

'You found him?' Robin took a step forward. His bow was lowered, but his hand remained within range of his sword. 'Or he found you?'

'Don't be so suspicious Robin, he's just a child.' Marion gestured towards the welcoming flames. 'We're pleased to meet you, Alwin. Would you like to sit by the fire?'

Stuttering and amazed to find himself in the company of Herne's most devoted servants, Alwin mumbled, 'Th… th… thank you, my Lady.'

The outlaws sat back down, all except for Tuck, who returned to preparing breakfast, as Much patted the ground next to him; inviting a hesitant Alwin to sit with him.

Robin spoke to Much, but he watched Alwin. 'What's the story, Much?'

'I found Alwin running through Sherwood while I was hunting for tonight's supper. He was calling to Herne and talking about a ritual.'

Robin was surprised, 'Herne?'

'Yes, and Gisburne was hunting him. Hunting Alwin I mean, not Herne.'

Will, who'd previously lost interest in the arrival of another mouth to feed before he'd had *his* breakfast, snapped his head up. 'Gisburne?'

'He wants to take Alwin to France.'

'For a rest?'

'Be quiet, Will.' Marion interrupted, 'Alwin, can you tell us why Gisburne was hunting you?'

Alwin studied his surroundings. He'd heard so much about these men and the Lady Marion, and now he was here with them. He couldn't help thinking that Herne had sent him to them for a reason. 'Well, um…'

Robin gave him a reassuring nod, 'It's alright. You can tell us.'

With a shy smile, Alwin began his tale. 'Gisburne came to my village. To Waterford. I was frightened because we don't get soldiers come to us very often. I heard him talking to his soldiers.'

Robin poked a stick into the fire, making the blaze crackle. 'What did he say?'

Alwin closed his eyes to try and picture the scene perfectly and capture every word he could remember. 'That the king wants men to fight in France. The soldiers said that I'd do. I don't think Gisburne liked me talking to my tree.'

Scarlet's complaint of 'Oh great, he's mad. Talking to trees—' was silenced by Nasir.

'Shh! Listen.'

Keeping his voice calm so as not to frighten the boy further, Robin said, 'Gisburne doesn't like anything he doesn't understand, Alwin. Did you hear the soldiers saying anything else?'

'Only about the king wanting fighting men. I think Gisburne is the one collecting them. I don't know… I was scared. I ran away… But I didn't have time to finish my ritual and—'

Not waiting to hear about the Waterford boy's ritual, Robin got to his feet. The others quickly followed, as he asked, 'Did Gisburne have a cart with him, Alwin?'

'I think so. I couldn't see clearly, but I'm sure I heard one.'

Working out what Robin had already guessed, Will checked for the dagger he kept tucked up inside his tunic. 'Gisburne could have half the men in the county ready to get slaughtered by now.'

Alwin's cry of, 'Slaughtered?!' echoed through the trees.

'Will!' Marion shouted, 'Honestly! He's just a boy.'

Mumbling, Scarlet shrugged out an apology, 'Well he could have. You know what Gisburne is like.'

'We have to go. Now.' Robin gathered a fistful of arrows and packed them into his quiver. As the others did the same, Alwin shuffled nervously by the fire.

Robin came to Nasir, 'Can you find them?'

'You want me to track the cart.' Speaking in his slightly clipped English, the Saracen sheathed his two curved swords into their scabbards. 'A pleasure.'

As Nasir jogged into the trees, followed by the outlaws. Alwin hung back before following. 'What's happening Much?'

Much put his finger to his lips to indicate they should remain quiet. 'We're going to stop Gisburne doing whatever he's doing, cos it's bound to be something wrong.'

'Oh. Good.'

Little John gave the newcomer a wink. 'I just wish we'd had time for breakfast first.'

Oh, I said
Sir John gave the twenty...
waiting a pleasure for you...

CHAPTER FIVE

Crossing the forest floor on silent feet, Nasir picked up the cart's trail. Stopping every now and then to make sure he hadn't made a mistake and was following the wrong path, he had soon led his friends to the road that connected Nottingham to Newark and beyond.

Nasir slowed to a walking pace, listening to the birdsong overhead as he checked his position once more. 'They have been here.'

A few hundred yards later, the Saracen stopped again and pointed along the road ahead of them. 'Just ahead. See?'

The outlaws peered into the distance in time to see a wagon being drawn along the road by two horses.

Robin studied the scene ahead, 'Six guards plus Gisburne, plus one man driving the cart.'

Nasir gestured to the wagon, 'It is heavy on its wheels. There must already be men inside.'

Scarlet snarled, 'Gisburne didn't waste much time, did he? We can only be four miles south of Waterford. Men from the next village, eh John?'

'Aye, and I'd bet he's grabbing any men walking along the forest road and chucking them in the cart as well. Next stop France!'

'Whatever it is we're going to do to stop him, Robin, we need to do it quick.' Scarlet glared into the distance, 'That cart is slow, but it is moving.'

'We'd better stop it in its tracks then.' Indicting his intentions with a wave of his arms, Robin issued his instructions. 'Marion, John, Nasir, you take the left side. Will, Tuck, we'll take the right. Ready?'

The chorus of 'Yes, Robin' from Marion and Tuck was joined by an 'Aye' from John, a nod from Nasir, and a growl of impatience from Scarlet.

'Well come on then, Robin!'

Robin gave Will a warning look. 'Once you're in position, wait for my signal.'

'As if I wouldn't wait.'

Not wanting to hold things up further, Much spoke quickly, 'What about me, Robin?'

'Stay close but undercover. Look after Alwin.'

'Okay, Robin. You can count on me.'

With a reassuring tap of Much's shoulder, Robin moved quietly to the other side of the road, followed by Scarlet and Tuck. Meanwhile, Marion, John and Nasir increased their pace as they wove through the cover of the trees on the opposite side of the road, making sure they stayed level with their comrades.

Hanging back to give the others a head start, Much then waved for their guest to follow him.

His expression grave, Alwin continued to talk to himself as they moved, 'Herne protect my new friends and—'

Much, anxious about being overheard, appealed to his new friend. 'Shhh! Please, Alwin. We must stay quiet.'

Mouthing an apology, Alwin dropped his voice. 'Herne protect us from—'

Still able to hear Alwin far too clearly for them to stay safely undetected, Much abruptly swung round to try to talk to the boy. He needed to make him understand how dangerous making any noise could be. Unfortunately, Alwin hadn't been paying attention to anything but the prayer he was uttering to the Lord of the Trees, and he walked straight into Much. Twisting his ankle in the process,

Alwin toppled backwards into some low-hanging branches.

'Ahhh!'

Much whipped his head from left to right in panic, 'Alwin! We must be quiet. If Gisburne's soldiers hear you, we could all be killed.'

Appalled that he might have put the others in danger, the boy pleaded, 'It's because I haven't done my ritual to the forest for Herne to keep us all safe. Anything could happen if I don't finish it.'

Unsure how to reason with the boy, Much said, 'Alwin, Robin is Herne's son. He is already protected. Please just follow me. And be quiet. We *have* to stay hidden near to the others in case they need our help.'

Level with the wagon from the castle, Robin couldn't see the outlaws across the road. He smiled to himself; that meant they were really close.

Gisburne, arrogant as ever, turned his head neither left nor right as he rode, his back straight, his chin held high—every bit the son of a Lord. The son of an Earl, Robin thought, thanking Herne that

Guy was at least unaware of the fact that a cruel twist of fate had granted them the same father, but different mothers.

The soldiers riding with the sheriff's steward, however, were more wary, each casting apprehensive glances into the trees as they trundled alone.

Robin kept moving with them, Scarlet and Tuck on his heels. The road ahead was slightly narrower than where they were now. Judging that would be the best place to stage his ambush so he and his followers could melt away into the forest if necessary (and there was less chance of having to kill a soldier who was simply doing his job), Robin held his nerve as they continued to shadow Gisburne's men.

The moment the tree cover was at its most dense and the road thinned, Robin gave a loud shout. 'Now!'

In an instant, the thundering footsteps of six outlaws blended with the heavy fall of hooves and the rusty squeak of the overloaded cart's wheels.

'Captain!' Gisburne yelled as three outlaws appeared from either side of the road, surrounding the cart with drawn bows.

It was already too late to draw his sword, so all the captain could do was order the party to halt. The wagon's wheels skidded as they were yanked to a stop, the horses whinnying in protest. The sound of men's voices from within, called out in fright, adding to the flash of chaos, which quickly subsided into an uneasy hush.

Taking a step forward, Robin aimed his arrow at Gisburne's heart.

As Guy watched the man he feared more than any other, he hissed quietly to the nearest soldier, 'Whatever happens, if you get a chance, shoot Hood.'

'My Lord.'

Satisfied his order had been delivered, Gisburne barked at the top of his voice, 'What do you want, Wolfshead?'

'Let the men in the cart go.'

'They are prisoners. I will do no such thing.'

Robin gave a theatrical sigh, 'Perhaps the arrow I'm pointing at you has become invisible? Do you want me to let go of it so we can find out?'

As the horse's hooves shuffled against the road, the tension in the air doubled.

Receiving no response from Gisburne, Robin spoke again, 'They might be your prisoners, but they aren't criminals, are they? What did they do?'

'I don't have to explain myself to you, outlaw.'

'My bow arm is feeling remarkably tired, Guy. Now, let... them... go.' Robin eased his bowstring back another inch, the arrow quivering against its nock.

'Captain!' Gisburne redirected his anger from the outlaw to his chief guard.

The captain shouted to the nearest two soldiers, who were looking far too afraid for their superior's liking, their horses pawing at the ground beside the cart's doors. 'Free the prisoners.'

There was a circling of horses as the chosen soldiers dismounted to carry out their master's wishes. John and Scarlet moved with them, their arrows trained on the men's backs while they undid the unwieldy bolts and the cart doors creaked open.

'Out!'

Eight men jumped from the covered wagon onto the road. They instantly began rubbing their eyes as the daylight hit them.

Robin, his bow not wavering from its potential target, called to Tuck, 'Check they aren't hurt.'

'Certainly Robin.' With one eye on the drama in the middle of the road, Tuck beckoned to the men. 'Over here you lot.'

As the friar stepped into the trees, the villagers followed in a rush of hasty footsteps. Tuck's jovial tone could be heard through the trees as he took charge. 'Wave your arms and limbs if you still have them.' He chuckled to himself, 'The Lord has spared you, now off you go. Head home, quickly now.'

Tuck's good humour dissolved as the men disappeared, and he stepped back into the clearing, his bow drawn and ready. 'No harm done, Robin.'

Taking a step closer to Gisburne, and with Nasir for protection at his heels, Robin said, 'It's time to explain yourself. Get off your horse.'

Dismounting slowly, Guy remained belligerent. 'I don't have to tell you anything.'

Unmoved by the temper of his enemy, Robin stepped closer. 'You can tell me... or you can tell Nasir. Which is it to be?'

The movement of the Saracen had been so swift that he was behind Gisburne, with a dagger at his throat, before anyone realised he'd moved. 'Hello, Sir Guy. A pretty blade, don't you think?'

Robin, internally impressed by the fact that Gisburne hadn't so much as flinched, said, 'If I ask him to, my friend here will show you how sharp he keeps his weapons. Won't you, Nasir?'

'It would be my pleasure.'

'Curse the lot of you.' Gisburne spat out.

'You can curse us all you like, Guy, but you are still going to have to tell us what you are up to.'

With hate and resentment pouring from every word, Gisburne said, 'I'm doing what King John has asked of me.'

'Ahh,' Robin relaxed the tension on his bowline a fraction, 'So, it's true. John does want more men to fight in France.'

Suspicion dripped from Gisburne's tongue, 'How did you know?'

'Never mind how.' Robin thought for a moment. 'I can't imagine that King John, for all his faults, has ordered you to kidnap villagers or travellers from the roadside.'

Aware of the close press of the dagger, Gisburne gulped, 'I'm not telling you anything else. I—'

Will Scarlet had had enough. Suddenly his always bubbling anger boiled over, and rang across the clearing, 'Gisburne! We haven't had breakfast yet, and I am *very* hungry. Just tell us what we want to know before I find something else to chew on, other than Tuck's stew!'

Stepping backwards, and immediately wishing he hadn't for the blade at his throat hadn't wavered, Gisburne shouted just as angrily. 'It's the sheriff. He doesn't want the King's recruiter in Nottingham. The sooner we have the men D'Marelle needs to send to France, the sooner he'll be gone.'

Scarlet felt his anger turn to ice in his veins, as he spoke a name that he hadn't heard uttered in years. 'D'Marelle?'

Robin gave Will a sidelong glance, 'I know that name. I've heard he's a brutal man.'

Gisburne grunted, 'I'm collecting a tax of people to keep him and the king happy.'

As his master spoke, the soldier who'd been instructed to shoot at Robin edged forward, raising his crossbow.

Unaware of the approaching threat, Robin said, 'You can tell De Rainault that I don't appreciate this new tax. I will be treating it like all the other unreasonable taxes King John asks of his people. Can you remember all that, Gisburne?'

About to lower his bow, Robin went cold as Marion yelled out an abrupt warning, 'Robin! Behind you!'

Swinging around, Herne's Son's bow fired, finding its mark with brutal accuracy as the soldier hit the ground.

Notching a new arrow, a furious Robin whirled back to an equally incensed Gisburne. 'I hope you haven't told any other soldiers to risk their lives by sneaking up on any of us. I don't want to kill another one. I didn't want to kill *him*!'

Gisburne, his face crimson with disappointment at another failed attempt to slay the outlaw, hissed, 'You should be more careful, Wolfshead. One day, you'll put a foot wrong and I'll—'

Interrupted by the sound of booted feet approaching from the side of the road, Gisburne gaped as familiar figure came into view—with Much in close pursuit.

Alwin waved a hand out before him in startled panic, his overly loud whisper clear for all to hear, 'That's Guy the Gamekeeper!'

Much pulled at Alwin's sleeve, trying to get him to go back undercover. 'Shh! We know that!'

Gisburne's horse began to stamp, pulling at the rein its master held, as the outlaws closed around Much and Alwin, forming a ring of protection.

'So, the heathen boy from Waterford... I see your taste in company has not improved, Huntingdon.'

Robin signalled to Nasir to lower the dagger. 'I think you should leave, Gisburne. Now. Do not forget to give De Rainault my message.'

Leaping into his saddle, Gisburne gave Alwin a hard, cold stare full of hate, 'Captain! We are leaving.'

As one unit, the soldiers accelerated into a gallop. With no weight to hold it steady as it was dragged behind them, the empty cart skittered precariously along the track.

Relaxing their weapons, Much rushed to Robin's side, 'I'm sorry. I tried to keep Alwin back, but he wanted to make sure he could see you.'

Alwin, his face a picture of concern, asked, 'Did I do something wrong?'

Giving the boy a reassuring smile, Marion said, 'Of course not.'

'That's good.'

As the outlaws walked back into the safety of the trees, they chatted quietly. All but Scarlet; hanging back a little, he appeared to be lost in thought.

'Are you alright, Will?' Marion stopped so he could catch up with her. 'You look like you've seen a ghost.'

'I've met D'Marelle before, that's all.'

Hearing Will's muted claim, Robin slowed his pace, 'Is he as bad as his reputation makes him out to be?'

'Worse.'

Seeing the sadness that flashed in Scarlet's eyes, Marion asked, 'How do you know him?'

Scarlet gave a defeated shrug. 'I fought in France, didn't I. D'Marelle was the monster who sent me there.'

CHAPTER SIX

The sound of persistently trickling water grew louder as the outlaws approached the edge of the village of Waterford.

The sun shone through the clouds, lifting Alwin's spirits as he dashed ahead of the outlaws, towards his home.

Dora's head peeped through the open door. Wary, her complexion was pale until she saw her son running towards her.

'Alwin!' Flinging her arms wide open, two points of colour lit up Dora's cheeks as she rushed forwards. Her apprehension at seeing her son with strangers diminished as she saw the grin on Alwin's face. 'Oh, thank goodness.'

Struggling to speak against the ferocity of his

mother's hug, Alwin mumbled into her shoulder, 'That's Much behind me. He's my friend, and so is Robin Hood too.'

'Robin Hood?' Dora's tired eyes sparked as she stepped back to take a proper look at her son, scanning him from head to toe, reassuring herself that all his limbs were where they ought to be. 'You are very welcome, Son of Herne. I'm Dora.'

Giving her a short bow, Robin said, 'I am pleased to meet you, Dora.'

'Thank you, Robin. Thank you *all* for bringing my boy home.' She raised her arms as if to engulf them all. 'I'm so grateful, but you see, the thing is…'

Alwin, excited to be home and full of relief to find his mother safe from harm, hopped from one foot to the other. Gesturing for Much to follow him, he led the young outlaw across the garden, jumping around as if he was an overexcited puppy. 'This is my special tree.'

Much peered upwards into the arms of the oak tree. Coloured strips of material and ribbon blew in the wind, while groups of loose twigs and pebbles sat snugly between the thicker branches and the trunk. 'It's umm... very nice.'

Shinning up into his tree, Alwin spoke with pride, 'I keep everyone safe from up here. This is where I do my ritual to the forest. First I tap the trunk with a stick three times and then...'

Robin remained uneasy. They'd restored a stolen son to his mother, but his instincts told him something else was wrong. 'You were going to tell us something, Dora?'

'I was.' She paused as if reluctant to speak before admonishing herself. 'Where are my manners? Ale. You'd like some ale after such an adventure this morning?'

Letting her gather her thoughts and knowing the others would be glad of a drink, Robin thanked Dora. 'That would be most welcome.'

Making her way to the cottage door, Dora beckoned them, 'Perhaps you'd like to come inside.'

Robin and Marion followed the woman into the small house, gesturing for the others to follow.

It would be a tight squeeze in the little home, but Robin had a feeling that everyone was going to want to hear what their host had to say.

Picking up a ceramic jug of weak ale, Dora gestured to her four beakers, 'Forgive me, but this is all we have. Would you mind sharing?'

Marion put her hand on the older lady's shoulder, 'Of course not. You are kind to offer us refreshment.'

'I'm sorry I don't have more to offer you, my Lady. Things have been hard since my husband died.'

'What happened to him?'

Concentrating on pouring the ale rather than looking at Marion's sympathetic eyes, Dora said, 'He went into the forest one day, two years ago, and never came home. It was winter and the harvest had been poor. We were desperate for food so... well... anyway, some foresters caught him poaching rabbits. You can guess the rest.'

Tuck crossed himself. He knew many who'd suffered at the hands of the instant sentencing and quick justice that Gisburne and his men employed. 'God rest his soul.'

'Thank you, Friar.' Dora sighed, 'That's when Alwin's ritual started.'

The sound of Alwin chanting in his tree could be faintly heard as it wafted through the open kitchen door.

Robin took a drink as he listened to the sing-song words floating across the garden. 'He talks to Herne?'

'Yes. Alwin is afraid that if he goes into Sherwood without doing his tree ritual, then he'll get killed too. It helped at first, so I didn't mind. But now—he has become so reliant on it.' Dora paused, 'I've tried to stop him, but it's become part of him. If only he'd pray to Herne quietly, inside where it's safe, so he wouldn't frighten the villagers. They keep away from us now.'

Disapproval crossed Robin's face. 'The other villagers living in Waterford don't help you now your husband's gone?'

Shaking her head, Dora sank onto the bench that ran along the kitchen table. 'The ritual worries them. They talk of witchcraft. I know Alwin isn't the sharpest lad, but he has a good soul. There isn't an evil thought in his head.'

Sitting next to Dora, Marion said, 'It's natural you should worry about him.'

'Well,' Dora pulled herself together, and turned to face Robin, 'it's all of us I'm worried for now.

I wasn't here when the soldiers stole Alwin away from me. I was in the village. The first I knew of his fleeing into Sherwood was when I got to the other side of the ford in time to see soldiers riding away. My Lord Gisburne was there, cursing someone he called "That wretched Waterford boy", I knew it had to be Alwin and I knew he was in trouble, but also that he'd escaped a worse fate. I searched the house and garden and up his tree, but Alwin was gone. I was about to go back to the village to ask for their help, and undoubtedly suffer their jibes about my son not being right in the head, when the soldiers appeared.'

Robin and Will jumped to their feet. Before Tuck had managed to un-wedge his girth from between the bench and the table, Robin was already issuing instructions. 'Scarlet, get Much. Nasir, check there's no one watching the house.'

Will and Nasir were out of the door in seconds, their daggers to hand, their senses alert.

Turning back to Dora, Robin spoke more gently. 'Can you tell us what happened, and how long ago?'

'You missed my Lord Gisburne by no more than ten minutes. He was so enraged at Alwin slipping through his fingers that he took them all. *All* our men folk.'

Little John slammed a hand against the table, making Dora flinch, 'Swine!'

Robin nodded, 'I doubt that's all he was angry about. He must have swung his soldiers round as soon as we were out of sight. Come on.'

As the others strode from the kitchen into the garden, Marion placed a calming hand over Dora's. 'Be strong for a little longer, Dora. We'll sort this out.'

Robin joined Will and John beside the ritual tree as Nasir returned from a quick scout of the immediate area. 'No one watches.'

A confused Much came to Robin's side. 'What's happening?'

Robin was about to explain when Dora, her face pale once more as the joy of her son's return became tainted by the knowledge that if Alwin had been taken then the rest of the villagers would have been spared, blurted out, 'If it hadn't been for Alwin's ritual, then perhaps he wouldn't have—'

Laying a hand on her shoulder, Robin shook his head. 'It wasn't Alwin's fault. It was Gisburne's. We'll get the villagers back. I promise.'

Giving Dora a parting hug, Marion said, 'Trust us, Dora. Look after yourself and Alwin.' Turning so she could see the tree where the boy was sat, his legs swinging happily over the edge of a branch, Marion added, 'We'll be back soon.'

As soon as they were out of earshot of Waterford, Scarlet rounded on Robin, his temper flaring, 'And how the hell are we going to do that then? Get the men back?'

Robin gave Will a determined look, 'We'll think of something, Scarlet. We have to.'

CHAPTER SEVEN

Robin took the bowl containing his late breakfast from Tuck as the outlaws sat back around the campfire. 'Thanks, Tuck. I'm starving.'

'Not as hungry as those poor wretches from Waterford, I suspect.'

'Aye,' John unfurled his long legs, and stretched them towards the flames. 'They'll be in Nottingham castle by now.'

As the friar continued to pass bowls of stew around the group, Scarlet tucked into his meal. Speaking through a mouthful of fish and herbs, he grumbled, 'Which means it's hopeless.'

'They're safe enough for a while.' Robin chewed thoughtfully. 'The sheriff won't risk sending King John damaged soldiers. He's already pushing his luck presenting D'Marelle with untrained villagers instead of hardened criminals.'

Scarlett nodded fervently. 'You'd better believe it. D'Marelle's temper is quicker to fire than a crossbow.'

Shivering beneath the shadow of the trees, wishing they could occasionally make camp in a place where the sunshine could pierce through the trees canopy, Marion pulled her shawl around her shoulders. 'Surely D'Marelle will curb his tongue in the sheriff's company.'

A harsh, humourless laugh escaped Scarlet's throat, 'I've seen D'Marelle order a man's death just cos he was shaking with fear before embarking for battle. Only a fool isn't afraid of war! I tell you, he'll kill the Waterford men there and then when he sees how scared they are.'

'He won't.' Robin spoke with a finality that most men wouldn't argue with. But Will Scarlet wasn't most men.

'And I'm telling you he is perfectly capable of—'

'Stop it you two.' Marion threw a handful of kindling at the pair of them. 'Squabbling isn't going to help anyone. D'Marelle isn't even in Nottingham yet, is he? So, we have to stop him on his way to the castle. It's obvious!'

'Marion's right. He's bound to go directly to the castle to collect his prisoners from the sheriff.'

'No need to sound so surprised, Robin.' Marion was indignant, 'I do have good ideas sometimes you know.'

Much groaned, 'You two aren't going to argue as well, are you?'

Speaking as one, Robin and Marion chorused, 'Of course not.' And then laughed at their unintentional symmetry.

A rare peace descended on the group as they all applied themselves to their meal, the only sound being the scrapping of wooden bowls as all traces of Friar Tuck's cooking disappeared. Only when he'd given up hope of extracting anymore food from his bowl, did Little John bring them back to the problem at hand.

'It makes sense to capture the wagon once the villagers are back inside it. When they are released from the gaol and are sent out of Nottingham again.'

Nasir nodded, 'It's too dangerous to break into the castle.'

'I agree.' Robin passed his bowl back to Tuck.

'I know you're right, but I don't like having to wait. Not this time.' Slamming a fist into his palm in frustration, Scarlett hissed, 'I don't want those villagers anywhere near D'Marelle, Robin. They might go hungry and be afraid under the sheriff's care—or lack of care—but at least he's just a bully. D'Marelle's evil.'

Resisting the temptation to remind Scarlet that he didn't *ever* like waiting for anything, Marion said, 'Then I suggest you calm down and get to D'Marelle *before* he reaches the castle.'

Will growled, 'He isn't exactly going to walk up to the castle on his own you know, Marion. What do you expect us to do, tap him on the soldier and ask him to come into the forest for a chat?'

Robin's body tensed as the mood around the fire darkened, 'Don't speak to Marion like that. Now, you apologise—'

'You're right. Sorry, Marion.' Stabbing his dagger into the ground between his feet, Scarlet held up a consolidatory hand. 'But Robin, how could you promise Dora we'll get the villagers back? We can't ever promise. We can only try our best.'

Marion laid a palm on her friend's shoulder, 'Come on, Will. Robin has never let you down.'

'I know. But one day our best isn't going to be good enough.' He pulled the dagger free and wiped the blade. 'It ain't me I'm worried about... Sorry, Robin, it's just, that man...' Will's voice faded off before he sat a little straighter. Taking comfort in the concerned faces of his friends, he carried on with his tale.

'I don't talk about France because... well... some of the things I saw...' Will hung his head in disbelief at his long-suppressed memories. 'And it was *his* fault. D'Marelle! If it hadn't been for him, I wouldn't have been there to see them horrors in the first place.'

Robin leaned forward, speaking softly, 'Do you want to talk about it?'

Self-conscious, not used to bearing his soul, Will spoke as if his mind was elsewhere. 'D'Marelle. He always overloads the ships he sends to France. Ships are expensive to sail...'

Will's voice trailed off again, lapsing into a tense hush until Marion said, 'Go on. It will help.'

Resigned and quiet, Will spoke with the bitterness of incomprehension at the deeds of others. 'D'Marelle doesn't go to France himself you know. He just sends others there to die. The boats... they're cheap and small. They don't always make it across the sea to France.'

Little John's voice was laced with regret. 'You saw a boat go down?'

Scarlet's eyes reflected the horrors he'd lived

through so long ago. 'I couldn't swim back when this happened. Hardly any of us could. I couldn't save...' His words snagged in his throat and Tuck passed him a cup of ale. He drank it down in one go before carrying on.

'We were still in sight of Lincolnshire. Two ships left together. I was on one, the other—' Will punched his fist against his own leg, but he was so wrapped in his memories that he felt no pain. 'D'Marelle saw the other ship sinking. He *saw* the men drowning! They were dying right in front of him. *In front of me.* They were yelling for help with their last breaths...' He paused momentarily and then looked directly at Robin's concerned face. 'He could have sent out rowing boats to save them. And do you know what he did, Robin?'

'Nothing?'

'Worse than nothing. Later, I learned that the few wretches from the lost ship who did make it back to shore were bundled straight onto another vessel. Their clothes soaking; they must have been terrified. I heard there were grown men—soldiers who'd seen death a-plenty—pleading to serve in the blood bath of Scotland instead of France. *Anything* to avoid going to sea again... If only I'd been able to swim.'

Pouring his friend another drink, Robin understood Will's helpless rage. 'You couldn't have saved them.'

Sipping his drink, Scarlet didn't hear what Robin had said as he went on with his tale. 'Some of the men who'd been on the ship with me leapt into the water to try and rescue their friends, but they were lost to the sea too. It was ice-cold and the current was strong. Their faces...' He turned his face to Robin's, 'Even when the sea overwhelmed them, I could feel their panic.'

'You might have been lost too, Will. Think how many lives you're saved with us since then. All those men and women walking free because you prevented them from being unjustly executed or thrown into prison to simply rot away.'

Scarlet shuddered at the strength of his memories. 'The men in the water... it was like watching leaves being sucked into a whirlpool. They didn't stand a chance.'

Raising his eyes, looking straight at Robin, Will said, 'You always say nothing's forgotten, and you're right. But sometimes... I just wish I could forget.'

A dense stillness spread over the camp. Not even the flames of the fire guttered as they burnt into lumps of wood and moss.

It was Much who eventually broke the tension. 'Didn't your ship stop to help the men, Will?'

Smiling at his young companion, once so naive but now grown into the realities of mankind's cruelty, Scarlet said, 'It just kept going. It was a long time before we were far enough away to escape the cries of the drowning men. Then, when the pleas for help finally ended, the silence was worse.'

Will paused, as the enormity of his tale sank in. His sadness of what happened quickly turned back into the fiery hate that burned him inside and made him who he was.

'That's why I hate D'Marelle, Robin.' He snarled. 'I *hate* him.'

CHAPTER EIGHT

Market day in Nottingham was always a boisterous affair. Today, with the sun brightening the sky, a variety of carts, horses, people on foot, both traders and shoppers alike, crowded through the gates of the already heaving streets. Everyone was ready to enjoy the first market of the year not to be tinted with a layer of frost. Calls of greetings rang out, as old friends shouted to make themselves known to each other. Guards barked orders back and forth as they checked the contents of every cart that was queuing to enter the city. The barking dogs and the squawking of chickens, bundled in baskets ready to be sold, combined with the honk of geese that were hurdled together just inside the city walls. It all provided a deafening wall of bustling sound.

One hundred yards from the goose pen, Robin, Will, and Nasir watched and waited.

Shielded from the city gates by a disused stable, Scarlet turned to Robin. 'Well, Naz and me ain't too recognisable under all the layers Marion insisted on bundling us into, but you Robin... That fair hair of yours is gonna get us caught if we're not careful.'

'I'll put my hood up.'

'Yeah, cos you never do that normally.' Will was worried. 'If just one sharp eyed informant or soldier spots you...'

'Let's hope people are too busy shopping to be paying attention to us then.'

'Yeah... hope. Brilliant plan.' Will rolled his eyes as Robin tucked a stray lock of golden hair under the cover of his hood.

The volume of noise from the market was increasing as the number of visitors to the city swelled. Standing with their backs flat against the stable, Will and Robin waited for the word to move from Nasir; who'd shinned up onto the roof for a better view of the gatehouse.

Restless, Will fought the urge to peep around the corner as the sound of the latest wagon to draw up to the gate was punctuated by the shout of 'Halt' from the guard on duty.

'Hurry up, hurry up.' Will's impatience grew as he heard the cart move on again, and another trundle into its place to the front of the queue. 'D'Marelle, where the hell are you?'

'Shh!' A sharp warning from Nasir, was followed by the arrival of his boots in front of their eyes as he lowered himself to the ground. 'The next cart is a prison wagon. It comes to the gates now.'

Mindful of Will's warning about his hood, Robin pulled it tighter over his head as he moved out of the shadows so he could see Nottingham's main entrance for himself. 'Is that D'Marelle, Will?'

Behind Robin, Scarlet spoke with grim satisfaction, 'That's 'im. He must have collected some other poor sods on the way here. See how low the wagon hangs on its axles?'

Robin murmured his agreement as Will whispered, 'D'Marelle is the one on the grey horse just ahead of the cart. He's older and fatter, but that's him alright. Can you see what's he doing, Naz?'

'Talking to the gate guards.' Nasir moved back against the wall of the stable. 'Market day is making it busy. He is having to take his turn to go through. This is good for us, but it's making him cross.'

Robin checked to make sure his dagger was in easy reach. 'Stick to the plan. We need to try and separate D'Marelle from the others before he disappears into the castle.'

'Yeah, we know' Scarlet stroked the top of the dagger that he'd hidden in the folds of this cloak, 'Come on, let's—' He froze before they'd travelled even one step. 'Wait. What's D'Marelle doing now?'

The guard in charge of gate duty was heartily wishing he was inside the castle guardroom sharing a jug of ale and a game of dice with his colleagues. Market day was always chaotic, but today the entire population of the shire appeared to have come to the city along with the good weather. Not only was it noisy, but the stench from the livestock was mixing with the stink from the midden behind the castle. Combined with the rather more pleasant smell of fresh baked bread and ale coming from the market itself, the result was making the guard feel hungry as well as making him need to gag. A headache formed, that didn't appear as if it would have the chance to ease anytime soon.

Now, to add it his problems, the honoured guest that the sheriff had warned him about was caught in the queue of ordinary people coming into the city, and he wasn't looking too pleased about it.

Sidestepping the hooves of a horse whose rider was having trouble controlling it in the confined space of the gully that ran to the gatehouse, the guard shouted to his men. 'Clear these people out of the way! I can see Lord D'Marelle trying to get through the gates. Quickly now. Make way!'

Elbowing men, women, and horses out of the way, the soldiers forced just enough of a gap between the stone walls and the mill of people for James D'Marelle to press his grey mount through the crowd, his men following with the laden cart.

Growling to the people around him, 'Out of my way.' D'Marelle edged forward. 'Move!'

Once he and his entourage reached the front of the queue, he glowered at the guard. 'Thank God for that. I was beginning to think we'd have to shoot our way into Nottingham.' Jumping from his horse, D'Marelle passed the bridle to the guard as another, clearly more senior, soldier strode forward.

'My Lord, D'Marelle. You are welcome.'

'You are the Sheriff of Nottingham's Captain of the Guard?'

'I am, my Lord. The High Sheriff and Sir Guy of Gisburne await inside, to take charge of the prisoners.'

'Do they now? Well, they're welcome to them.' He banged hard on the side of the wagon as it pushed past, causing muffled protests to come from inside. 'If I have to listen to one more whinging felon... They might be desperate men with nothing to lose, but the way they go on you'd think they'd rather go to gallows than France.'

The captain gestured for a party of men to come forward to escort the wagon into the castle. 'Some think there's little to choose between death and France, my Lord.'

'Are you this insolent to the sheriff?'

D'Marelle's reply had been sharp, and the captain hoped his men hadn't overheard the exchange. 'Forgive me, my Lord.'

'I might.' The older man peered into the captain's shrew-ish eyes, quickly taking measure of his ruthless ambition. 'Take the prisoners and my men to the castle. Inform De Rainault that I will join him later.'

Bowing, the captain took a step back to let D'Marelle pass. 'My Lord.'

Using the cries of the market stallholders shouting their wares and the general bustle of the shoppers as cover, the three outlaws left the shelter of the stable. Moving slowly towards the gate, Scarlet hung back a second time as the view of the gateway became less obstructed.

Robin frowned, 'Scarlet, come on. The soldiers are moving off, we have to move now!'

Will pointed straight ahead, his feet planted to the spot. 'Where's D'Marelle going?'

'Into the market.' Robin now understood why Will had stopped. This wasn't going to be the rush up to the castle steps, public kidnapping of the king's chief recruiter that they'd planned. 'He's sending his men into the castle, but he's not going with them.'

Suspicious of this, Will said, 'Makes our job easier, I suppose.'

Robin inched forward, keeping a watch in every direction as he got further from the safety of the stable and the forest border. 'Looks like he's going into the market alone. I wonder why?'

Will's eyebrows' rose in surprise. 'To do a bit of shopping?'

Nasir fixed his eyes on the grey-haired figure as he merged with the crowd. 'We move now.'

By this time an argument had broken out between the guards and the people trying to get inside the city walls. Neither side appeared to be making any progress. Taking advantage of the guard distraction, the three outlaws walked forward.

Slipping through the gap between a carter trying to get into Nottingham and the wall of the gatehouse, Robin said nothing until they were all safely inside the city. 'Don't kill D'Marelle as soon as he's within arm's reach, Will. We need to talk to him.'

Scarlet flashed a dangerous smile, 'As if I would.'

Following Nasir, trusting the Saracen's instincts and tracking skills even in the hubbub of the marketplace, Robin and Will obeyed when their friend gave the swiftest of hand signals, telling them to stop moving.

Pretending to be interested in a row of cooking pots for sale, they watched as D'Marelle, only two stalls ahead of them, relaxed before their eyes. He was greeting everyone politely, with hearty cries of 'Greetings' and 'Good day to you.'

Nasir's eyes narrowed. 'He seems different.'

As D'Marelle moved on, the outlaws continued to follow, picking their way discreetly through the crowd.

Robin was thoughtful, 'One face for the soldiers, another for everyone else.'

Nasir agreed, 'There is no swagger. No anger now.'

'Because he is unknown here, perhaps?' Robin observed with interest as the old solider exchanged a joke with a butcher who was enthusiastically skinning a rabbit. 'He can be someone else here, while he's away from the prying eyes of the king and his officials.'

Scarlet was unmoved. 'Don't be fooled, Robin. That man is one of the hardest human beings I've ever encountered.'

As D'Marelle walked away from the butcher's stall, Nasir led the others forward, before pausing again a few paces later, shielding their presence in the gap behind the rolls of fabric piled next to the stand of a travelling textile merchant. 'The recruiter is by the bread stall. He jokes with the women.'

'He is certainly enjoying himself.' Robin observed.

Scarlet shook his head, 'You'd never think to see him now that he sends people to hell for a living, would you?'

Walking faster, to keep up with D'Marelle who was now being buffeted along with the moving crowd, the outlaws were thankful their quarry was taller than average so they could easily see his crown of thick grey hair.

'He gets too far ahead.' Nasir increased his pace, 'We must hurry.'

Scanning the area with each step, Robin kept his eyes open for potential trouble. 'D'Marelle's heading for the ale stall. I've got an idea. You two stay close.'

Reaching out to Robin, Scarlet demanded, 'Hang on Robin, what are you doing?'

'Trust me but stay nearby.' With an extra tug of his hood, Robin hooked a few coins from his pocket and elbowed his way through a gathering of men who were already heading towards alcohol-thickened heads, despite the earliness of the hour.

With a shrug, Nasir edged to the opposite side of the stall, while Will remained a few steps behind Robin, his hand hovering over the handle of his dagger. He could see his old enemy clearly now. D'Marelle had an arm companionably resting on the stall's counter. He had the manner of a man who had all the time in the world, as he watched the two women within rush around with flushed exertion, filling tankards and checking that their supplies were going to last out the day.

'Excuse me, excuse me—' Robin banged a palm down on the counter, off-balance even when propped up at the bar, a belch escaping from his mouth as he tried to apologise to the man he stood swaying next to. 'Oh, I does alopo... applelo.... apooliji....' Robin spoke as clumsily as he moved; giving a half-hearted low bow to D'Marelle, who regarded him with patient amusement. 'What I is trying to say, is I is very sorry.' Robin added. He slapped D'Marelle on the back, heartily. 'Ahh... a soldier man. Let I get you a drink, m'friend.'

D'Marelle, inclined his head, 'Why, that's very civil of you.'

Realising what the outlaw's leader was up to, Scarlet pulled out his dagger, and, pressing his chest against the old soldier's back, hissed in his ear, '*He* may be civil. But I ain't.'

Stepping backwards in shocked surprise, trying to swivel around to see who'd spoken, D'Marelle's face flushed into hushed anger, 'What are you...?'

'Now, now, let's stay nice and quiet, my *Lord*.' Scarlet sneered as he uttered D'Marelle's title. Pressing his point home, Will angled the tip of his dagger through the folds of the recruiter's cloak, pushing just hard enough to make his weapon's presence felt.

The soldier tried to twist his head, but Will was ahead of him. 'No need to look down, D'Marelle. You already know I've slipped a blade under your cloak. And I think you'll find that my friend here has taken your own knife for safe keeping.'

There was a light swish of metal as Nasir threw the stolen knife from one hand to the other before stowing it away. 'It is a good knife.'

D'Marelle said nothing. There was no point in appealing to anyone for help. The barmaids had melted away, their sense of self-preservation strong, and the crowd, all but for the newly-arrived drunk with the hood—who seemed oblivious to everything but the beaker he was staring into, were mysteriously absent.

Scarlet gave a humourless grin. 'Now, be a good boy, D'Marelle, and walk with us to the gates. And keep your mouth shut.'

D'Marelle grunted as he levelled his eyes on Scarlet as if searching for a point of recognition.

Nasir tapped the folds of his jacket, beneath which he'd hidden the knife. 'That noise was a yes, I think.'

'Good enough.' Will flapped a hand towards the city gates, 'Come, my Lord, I'm thirsty, and I believe my friend offered you some ale.'

'Indeed I did.' Robin put down his tankard and stood up straight and still. 'But I didn't say where he'd be drinking it.'

CHAPTER NINE

The moment they'd left the market, Scarlet grabbed hold of D'Marelle's sword arm. He didn't let it go until he'd thrust their unwelcome guest to the ground beside the outlaw's campfire.

'You don't remember me, do you?' Scarlet sat next to the recruiter, playing his dagger between his fingers.

Taking the opportunity to examine his ardent captor for the first time, D'Marelle asked, 'Should I?'

'You sent me to France.'

D'Marelle gave a small shrug, 'I've sent a lot of men to France. I don't recall you. I'm glad you made it home again.'

Standing back from the fire Marion, spoke

quietly, 'He isn't what I expected, Robin. Something's happened to him.'

Robin slipped a hand into hers and gave it a light squeeze of agreement, before picking up a jug of ale and a beaker and approaching their visitor. 'I promised you a drink.'

Taking the ale, D'Marelle appeared wary but unafraid. 'You're Robin Hood, aren't you?'

'And you are Sir James D'Marelle. Chief recruiter for King John's French campaigns.'

A shadow cast over D'Marelle's face. 'For my sins.'

Scarlet's laugh came out like a bark. *'All* of them?'

Shooting Will a look that told him to keep quiet, Robin sat opposite D'Marelle. 'Your reputation precedes you. However, the man I saw in the market did not appear to be the same person I saw talking to sheriff's captain at the gate. It is as if you are play-acting. But which is the real you? The irate soldier or the cheerful market goer?'

'Asks the outlaw, the legend, and the Earl's son. You are also just one man.'

Robin held the old soldier's piercing blue gaze. 'You have not answered my question.'

Taking a draft of his ale, D'Marelle watched the gutter of the warming flames before him. 'I am becoming old. It takes more energy than it used to, to maintain my authority. Yet, I must continue to be seen to be in charge.'

'Perhaps,' Robin nodded, 'but there's more to it than that.'

'Isn't there always?' With a resigned sigh, D'Marelle spoke into the flames. 'I had a son. Richard. He was naive in the ways of the world. He talked to the trees and the birds.'

Nasir, whose eyes had been unwaveringly levelled on their guest since they'd reached the camp, said, 'There is peace to be found in talking to the birds.'

'So there is. I know that now, but then…' He paused, and lifting his gaze, spoke as if appealing to the group. 'I thought if I recruited Richard, it would make a man of him. A trip to France should have chased his childish ways from him. Instead…'

D'Marelle paused, his eyes clouding in despair as he thought of the son he had loved but couldn't understand. 'Oh, what's the point? Why did Richard waste time talking to tree Gods that don't exist when a sword would have given him all the help he needed?'

Much stood up, his expression defiant. 'But Herne does exist!'

'Not now, Much…' Marion laid a hand on her

young friend's shoulder. 'D'Marelle, your plan to make Richard grow into the man you wanted him to be—it didn't work, did it?'

'It did not. I truly believed that military service for his king would do my boy some good. Give him some backbone.'

Hearing the reluctance to go on in his voice, Marion coaxed, 'But?'

D'Marelle swallowed hard, 'It killed him. I might as well have struck the blow myself.'

Letting the man's words hang in the air for a minute, Robin said, 'I'm sorry to hear that. It doesn't excuse what's happening here though.'

Without appearing to have heard Robin, D'Marelle went on, 'When I got back to England, I was so incensed with myself, with the king, with the war, with England, with everything! I let my anger rule me. I was foolish. I did not exercise the caution which is wise in the presence of King John.'

Marion pushed him further, 'And?'

'I lost my temper and shouted at King John, demanding to be freed from the service of sending the sons of good men to their deaths.'

Little John's eyebrows rose so high they were almost hidden by his shaggy fringe. 'It's a miracle you still have your head.'

'My punishment was far worse than instant death. I am condemned to remain King John's chief recruiter. To travel up and down England rounding up men who hate me until fate intercedes and my death comes.'

Robin listened to D'Marelle with interest, but he hadn't lost sight of the reason that the recruiter was visiting Nottingham. 'Meanwhile, Robert de Rainault is sending his man, Guy of Gisburne, out to capture innocent men to add to the king's forces. A people tax in your name, D'Marelle!'

'A people tax?' The recruiter's expression of surprise was genuine. 'Nothing would surprise me about the Sheriff of Nottingham. I have not yet met the man, but his reputation for being lazy and underhand is widespread.'

Little John tussled a hand through his beard, 'That's our beloved sheriff alright.'

D'Marelle's shifted uncomfortably against hard earth. 'The new soldiers were supposed to be gathered by emptying the prisons around the county. It is only felons I've been instructed to send abroad.'

Robin clarified, 'Just *guilty* prisoners?'

'King John has asked for convicted men who otherwise face a life of imprisonment or the hangman's noose. It's a chance for them to work towards a pardon and freedom.'

Scarlet dug at the ground with the tip of his dagger. '*If* they live.'

Leaning towards the recruiter, Robin said, 'Gisburne has imprisoned every man of working age from the village of Waterford just because one boy annoyed him. There is not a felon amongst them.'

Scarlet began to wipe the earth from his dagger, 'He will have taken more men by now.'

Robin switched his full attention to their hostage. 'Scarlet is right. Gisburne will have gathered up others. Men that have committed no crime but are easy to scoop from the roadside.'

'Having had the dubious pleasure of Sir Guy's company prior to his time fighting in France, I can't say I'm surprised by his method of recruitment.'

Much turned to D'Marelle, 'You know Gisburne, then?'

'He fought for me in France,' D'Marelle's dared a glance at Scarlet, 'Many men did.'

Seeing that Will was about to launch into an argument about the treatment of English soldiers, Robin cut in. 'Answer me honestly, D'Marelle, should proven criminals be found to replace the villagers, would you agree to an exchange of men?'

'I would.' The recruiter nodded. 'I have been instructed to take fifty convicted criminals from the counties gaols. I simply need fifty fighting men.'

'With your help we could replace the villagers with criminals.'

'I do not have the luxury of time to take part in heroics, outlaw.'

Scarlet tipped the point of his dagger in D'Marelle direction. 'And very soon you won't have the luxury of walking if you don't help us.'

Robin leant forward, 'Your answer, my Lord?'

Reluctantly, knowing he was probably damned either way, D'Marelle agreed.

'Providing I have the fifty men the king asked the sheriff to find, it doesn't matter who they are.'

Pushing their advantage, Robin looked straight into their guest's eyes as he said, 'Can you imagine King John's reaction if he discovers the Sheriff of Nottingham tricked you into taking untrained farm workers from his fields? Men who work on his land, rather than criminals who cause only harm to his realm?'

D'Marelle ran a hand through his hair, 'Unfortunately, I can.'

CHAPTER TEN

The stones of Nottingham castle exuded a chill that didn't help the frosty atmosphere.

As the servants served food to the sheriff, D'Marelle regarded his hosts. He knew that neither Gisburne nor De Rainault believed he'd been exploring the market between delivering the future soldiers and arriving at the castle for such a long period of time.

Although he'd hardly enjoyed his encounter with the most notorious outlaws in the country, it filled him with private amusement that his current companions had no idea he'd met the King of Sherwood.

Leaning back so that a servant could add more pork to his plate, D'Marelle said, 'So, tell me,

Gisburne, are you still making doomed attempts to climb the social ladder?'

Not rising to D'Marelle's bait, Gisburne said, 'It's good to see you again too, my Lord.'

Switching his focus to the sheriff, D'Marelle asked, 'What say you, De Rainault? Is Sir Guy here destined for greatness?'

The sheriff found himself warming to their unwelcome guest. Since his brother, Abbot Hugo, had waltzed off on a pilgrimage a month ago, so he could avoid having to meet the latest bishop to tour the county, he'd missed having someone to taunt Gisburne with. 'Only in his head. More wine, my Lord?'

'Thank you, my Lord Sheriff.'

'Please, call me Robert.' The sheriff clicked his fingers, 'Gisburne, get us more wine.'

Grimacing, Gisburne replenished their cups.

'Thank you, Sir Guy.' D'Marelle toasted him, 'You make a fine wine-servant. Better with a flagon than with a sword on the battlefield, that's for sure.'

Gisburne grumbled under his breath, 'It would have been hard to see me with a sword on the battlefield from the safety of the English shoreline.'

The sheriff's interest was piqued. 'You've never told me about your experiences in France, Gisburne.'

'You've never asked me, my Lord.'

D'Marelle picked a chicken leg up off his plate. 'Too ashamed to talk about it, I shouldn't warrant.'

The sheriff laughed as he took another drink, 'Probably, my Lord.' He found he liked their visitor more with every sip of wine.

Laying down his knife, confident that De Rainault was drunk enough to be easily manipulated, D'Marelle went on, 'This talk of Sir Guy with a sword, brings us to the reason for my visit. Are my prisoners ready? The king's clerk reported that you would have no problem raising your fifty men once you'd emptied all the county gaols, including those at Newark.'

Gisburne made a small choking noise, but held his peace as the sheriff said, 'My dear James, you must understand, I was only visited by the clerk yesterday. As yet Gisburne has not managed to gather the numbers together.'

The recruiter tutted, 'Typical.'

'Newark is a long way, my Lord D'Marelle,' Gisburne snapped, 'Anyway, my Lord Sheriff said I shouldn't—'

Interrupting, the sheriff glared at his deputy. 'I *said* that the number of men the king requested will be ready soon.'

D'Marelle rose his cup in a toast to the occasion. 'I am delighted to hear it. I was concerned you would try and weasel your way out of your obligations, De Rainault.'

The sheriff spluttered against his cup, 'I must protest.'

'Must you? How tiresome.'

Gisburne barked out a sharp laugh, but it was cut short as D'Marelle underlined their position.

'If King John doesn't get the soldiers he has requested, he intends to send his less able officials to Normandy instead. You, De Rainault, are right at the top of his recruitment list.'

Instantly sober, the sheriff sat up straight. 'I beg your pardon.'

D'Marelle spoke with calm authority, savouring the worried glint to the sheriff's eyes. 'You can't be surprised, surely? With Nottingham's taxes regularly going astray, what would you have the king do? Your luck can't last forever, De Rainault.'

Leaning forward, as if he was offering friendly advice, the recruiter added, 'In fact, if I were you, I'd gather rather more men than the number John has requested.'

Sitting up again, D'Marelle slapped his palm against the table, making his dining companions jump. 'Win yourself some much-needed favour while you can, man.'

Weighing up the truth of what the recruiter was saying, the sheriff addressed his steward, 'Gisburne.'

'My lord?'

'You will ride to Newark at dawn.'

A crease of confusion appeared across Gisburne's forehead, 'But, my Lord, you said—'

'At dawn, Gisburne!'

CHAPTER ELEVEN

The captain of the guard had wisely held his peace when a furious Gisburne had arrived in the guardroom late the previous evening, announcing that he'd need a group of men and a wagon to leave for Newark at dawn.

Now, as they rode into the crisp morning, Gisburne's sense of injustice hanging around him like a shroud, the captain finally broke the tense silence. 'Waterford is ahead, my Lord. Newark should be in our sights before noon.'

'Good. The sooner we get the prisoners in that cart and back to Nottingham the better.'

The captain smirked, 'At least there's no need to stop at Waterford, my Lord. The cream of that crop has already been harvested.'

Gisburne grunted, 'Apart from the pagan boy.'

His voice as slick as goose fat, the captain said, 'It is galling he slipped through our fingers, my Lord.'

Giving his companion a sidelong look, Gisburne said, 'I wonder… Captain, slow your men.'

Speaking quietly, so that his words didn't travel on the stagnant dawn air, the captain asked, 'Do you want us to track the boy, my Lord?'

'No need, you blind fool. He's there, in his cursed tree.'

As his mounts slowed to a halt, the captain's eyes followed where his superior was pointing. 'So he is. The devil works early in the morning.'

Gisburne spoke out of the side of his mouth, 'Deploy your men. Go with them. I don't want to lose that tree rat this time.'

Accompanying three of his guards, the captain concentrated on the ribbon bedecked oak tree where a young boy sat, his legs swinging, his eyes closed, his lips chanting a melody worthy of any balladeer.

The soldiers were on Alwin before he'd noticed their approach. Scrambling to the end of the branch, he made to drop to the ground.

Yelling for his mother, Alwin squirmed out of the grip of the first soldier as a lunge was made for his legs, but in doing so he fell victim to the grasp of the other two who took a firm hold of his shoulders.

'NO! Let go!' Alwin kicked out at a fourth soldier.

The captain winced as the boy's boot connected with his jaw. 'Ouch! You'll pay for that!'

Alwin screamed as all four men pounced on him at once, dragging his resisting body towards the waiting cart.

'Mother. Herne. Help! Mother!'

There was a bang as the front door of the house crashed open, and Dora ran from within. 'Let him go!'

Outraged to see her son following in the footsteps of the men of Waterford, Dora dashed towards the cart, just in time to see the doors bang shut against Alwin.

'Alwin? No! Let him go!'

Safely out of reach, Gisburne laughed as the distraught woman set about his guards with her wooden spoon. 'Get off my boy!'

Gisburne would have stayed to enjoy the scene for longer, but he remembered that time was short. 'Stop attacking my men you stupid hag, or we'll take you into the King's service as well.'

The captain of the guard rubbed at the bruise forming on his chin. 'I bet the French would love her.'

Running to Gisburne's horse, Dora clasped her hands together as if in prayer. 'Please, my Lord. *Please* let my boy go!'

Gisburne's face creased into distaste. Speaking to his men as if Dora couldn't hear him, he commanded, 'Throw the female into the ford. We need to get to Newark.'

The captain grinned, 'Certainly, my Lord.' Without a backward glance, he spun on his heels and, pushing two palms hard against Dora's shoulders, sent her toppling backwards into the ford behind her.

Landing in the shallow water with a splash, Dora's cry of 'A curse on you, Guy of Gisburne,' followed her son's muffled cries as the cart disappeared into the distance.

'Alwin, oh Alwin.' Sobs rose in Dora's throat as she waded out of the water. Not delaying to even change into dry clothes, she scuttled into Sherwood.

'Robin. I must find Robin. Herne, please help me. Guide me to Robin Hood.'

Marion's hand became motionless in the process of collecting kindling wood. Her body had sensed the someone approaching before her ears picked up the sound of scurrying feet. Stepping into the cover of the trees, she waited to see who it was.

'Dora!'

'Lady Marion,' Dora wiped the tears from her cheeks, 'Thank goodness I've found you. It's Alwin. Gisburne has my Alwin.'

Her expression bleak, Marion took the other woman's hand. 'The others should hear about this too, come with me.'

Now that Dora had found who she'd been searching for, the energy that had kept her going deserted her, and she leant heavily against Marion as they walked to the camp.

The outlaws, who'd been sharpening their swords and daggers, stopped work as soon as Dora appeared.

Rushing forward, Robin took her hands, understanding at once what had happened. 'Gisburne has taken your boy.'

Fresh tears trickled down Dora's face as she sank to the forest floor. 'France. They want him to fight in France. He'll die. He's no fighter.'

Robin sat next to her, 'It's alright. We'll get him back. We already have a plan to free the other Waterford men.'

Dora looked far from convinced, 'But what about Alwin? Gisburne might not take him to join the others.'

Robin gestured to Tuck to bring their guest some food. 'We'll rescue Alwin.'

Thanking the friar as he passed her a hunk of bread, Dora's eyes lit with hope, 'How?'

'We'll find a way. Alwin won't be going to France.' Robin's eyes met Will's, silently warning Scarlet not to put any doubts into their guest's mind.

Dora's shoulders started to shake as the events of the day sank in. 'You promise?'

'I promise. You eat, rest, and then head home. We'll bring Alwin back as soon as we can.'

Returning to sharpening his weapons with John, Scarlet muttered, 'I wish Robin wouldn't keep making promises he might not be able to keep.'

Little John's manner was also grim. 'We'd better

make sure he does keep the promise then, hadn't we?'

Much picked up a pouch to fill with slingshot, 'John?'

'Yes, lad?

'Umm,' Much felt awkward as he asked, 'Alwin will be alright, won't he?'

Not wanting to lie, Little John ruffled a hand through Much's hair. 'We'll do our best.'

Looking more determined than either of the other men had ever seen him, Much said, 'Our very *very* best.'

CHAPTER TWELVE

The crossroads that divided the road connecting Newark and Nottingham with the route from Nottingham and Lincoln lay before the outlaws.

'This is it.' Nasir held up his hand, indicating for his friends to wait as he moved stealthily beyond the shelter of the trees.

Seconds later he was back. 'The road is clear.'

Robin turned to Much. 'D'Marelle said this is where he would collect the prisoners that Gisburne is bringing from Newark.'

'The men he's going to exchange for the Waterford prisoners?'

'Yes. Can you climb that tree and lookout for their approach?'

Once Much had hitched himself into the tree,

Robin called up to him, 'As soon as you spot *anyone*, make the birdcall Nasir taught you. If you see D'Marelle or Gisburne, then jump down at once to tell us.'

'Okay, Robin.'

Stood next to Robin, making sure her skirts were tucked safely into her belt so she didn't trip over them if they had to run, Marion said, 'At least what we learned from Dora after Alwin's capture tells us that D'Marelle did what you asked. He's cooperating with our plan.'

'And that De Rainault went for the bait.'

Scarlet laughed, 'Yeah, can you imagine the sheriff's face at the thought of being sent to France himself?'

Marion couldn't help but smile, 'Not to mention Gisburne's expression when he was ordered to ride to Newark and back in just one day.'

Little John chuckled. 'I bet his face was a picture, lass. I can just imagine…'

The sound of Much's bird call cut through the forest clearing. Robin moved to the foot of the tree, 'What can you see?'

'A wagon from Nottingham.'

Scarlet slipped a dagger from his belt, 'D'Marelle?'

'Umm…' Much edged further along the branch. 'Yes.'

Jumping down, Much joined the other outlaws as they waited undercover. The rumble of the approaching cart and accompanying horses was getting louder.

Robin nodded to his band, 'Draw your weapons, just to be safe. D'Marelle may well have done what we asked—'

Will finished Robin's sentence for him, 'But he might not.'

'We'll soon find out.' Robin pulled back his bow. 'Make yourselves ready.'

Crouching between Scarlet and John, the sound of the hooves beating against the ground matching the beat of his heart, Much murmured, 'Will?'

'What is it?'

'What's it like in France?'

'You're lucky you'll never know.' Giving Much a reassuring tap on the knee, Scarlet kept his eyes to the road. His voice was muted as he added, 'I hadn't known about D'Marelle's son, though.'

John, easing the muscles in his legs by stretching them out one at a time, said, 'His lad's death has altered him, I reckon. That's why he's helping us.'

Notching an arrow to his bow, Robin frowned.

'We have to trust him, Scarlet, or none of the villagers will get out.'

'You can trust him if you like. But, however changed he seems to be, I'm not convinced.'

'He's on his way here, isn't he?' Robin uttered a private prayer to Herne for help as he added, 'D'Marelle has done everything he promised so far.'

Mumbling, so that only John could hear, Will said, 'I don't know 'bout you, but I've never thought that *so far* was good enough.'

John was spared having to reply as Robin held up a hand.

D'Marelle and his guards were reining in the cart only a few strides from where the outlaws were waiting.

Making rather slower progress, Gisburne and his men trotted either side of a wagon full of prisoners extracted from Newark gaol, along with Alwin.

'I can see D'Marelle's party ahead, my Lord Gisburne.' The captain of the guard pointed towards the stationary group at the side of the forest road.

'Thank goodness.' Gisburne was relieved that D'Marelle had honoured his agreement to meet him on the road, thus saving him from having to transport the slow wagon all the way to Nottingham. 'Let's get rid of this lot and get back as fast as we can.'

Dismounting from his horse, D'Marelle stepped forward to greet Gisburne. 'Nice of you to turn up, Sir Guy.'

Without acknowledging the recruiter, Gisburne addressed his captain. 'Hand command of the wagon to these men.'

'Certainly, my Lord.'

Continuing to act as if D'Marelle wasn't there, Gisburne added, 'I have no problem dumping rubbish on a midden.'

Watching as the wagon's horses were unharnessed, their position ready to be taken up by two of D'Marelle's mounts, Gisburne finally spoke directly to the recruiter. 'I wish you a thoroughly unpleasant onward journey, my Lord. Come, Captain, the sheriff is waiting for us in Nottingham.'

There was an abrupt thunder of hooves and, only seconds later, Gisburne and his men were galloping into the distance.

From their hiding place, the outlaws tensed, ready to strike if D'Marelle showed any sign of breaking his promise to swap the prisoners.

Robin whispered, 'Nasir, can you make sure Gisburne really has gone this time.'

Having anticipated the instruction, Nasir was already halfway up the nearest tree, 'I can.'

Impatient to free Alwin, Much inched forward, but Little John put out a restraining hand and pulled him back. 'Hang on, lad. I know you want to get the boy out of there, but a bit longer won't make any difference.'

'He must be scared.'

'I'm sure he is, but we must wait.'

As soon as Nasir gave the all-clear, Robin called everyone together. 'You know what to do. Be careful.'

Then, striding into the open ground of the crossroad, his bow at the ready, but with the arrow aiming at the ground rather than the soldiers, Robin said, 'I'm pleased to see you, D'Marelle.'

The recruiter greeted the outlaw as his followers broke cover, 'I have explained the situation to my men. They won't stop you from freeing the villagers.'

Without wasting time, Robin issued instructions. 'John, Will, open the cart from Nottingham. Marion and Tuck, can you make sure no one is hurt? Nasir, Much, get Alwin out of the other cart.'

Rushing forward, Much had the cart's doors thrown open before Nasir had reached his side. 'Alwin? Alwin are you in here?'

Relief rang in his every word as the boy from Waterford scrabbled over the legs of the other captives towards daylight, 'Much? Is that you?'

'Yes, come on!'

'Oh, thank Herne.'

While Alwin dashed towards Much, Nasir checked to make sure only genuine felons from Newark remained in the cart. Meanwhile, John and Will had started to help the innocent men who'd been packed into the wagon from Nottingham to freedom. They'd been jammed into the cart so tightly, it was as if they were pigs off to slaughter.

'Waterford?' Scarlet levered a latest frightened looking man from the cart and pointed to Tuck and

Marion at the side of the road. 'Right, go over there then.'

'Out you come. NO, not you.' There was a hefty thump and a furious mouthful of curses as John shoved one man back inside, 'I know you! You're the sort of cutthroat that gives cutthroat's a bad name. You are certainly not from Waterford. Actually, I don't care where you're from, you're going to France.'

As the assembly of men on the edge of the forest grew, Tuck examined everyone for cuts and bruises, before Marion reported to Robin.

'No one appears to be hurt. Just grubby, shaken and hungry. The sooner they get back to Waterford, the better.'

'Thank you, Marion.' Robin gestured towards where Much and Alwin were sat together at the edge of the forest. 'Is he alright?'

Seeing Robin looking at him, Alwin ran across the road, with Much hot on his heels. 'Thank you, Herne's Son.'

Robin smiled as he took in the boy's grime-streaked face and filthy clothing. 'You are welcome.'

Much beamed, 'You're safe now.'

Seeing that John and Will had shut and relocked the cart door, and that Nasir, with the help of one of D'Marelle's men, was pushing the Newark wagon doors closed, Robin asked, 'Is that all from Waterford accounted for, Marion?'

'That's all of them.'

Tuck came to Marion's side, confirming what she'd already reported. 'There are not more than a few scratches on them, Heaven be praised.'

Relieved, knowing that a night in Nottingham castle prison would leave the villagers in a much worse condition, Robin waved a hand towards the trees. 'They should head back to Waterford straight away. Tell them to travel through Sherwood rather than using the road.'

Flapping his arms, as if he was herding geese, Tuck returned to the freed men. 'You heard Robin. Back to safety. Off home you go.'

As the villagers disappeared into the arms of the forest, Alwin tapped on Much's shoulder. 'Is it *really* safe now, Much?'

'Alwin! Why are you still here?' Much ran his eyes over the immediate area, searching for any other Waterford men that might have lingered. 'You should have gone with the others.'

'I wanted to stay with you.'

'Oh, well, I suppose it's alright. The recruiter man has all the soldiers he needs to go to France now.'

'Good.'

CHAPTER THIRTEEN

As Little John, Nasir, and Will left the genuine criminals in the care of D'Marelle's men, Robin un-notched his arrow and slung his bow over his shoulder. 'Thank you, my Lord. You did a good thing today.' He offered his hand to D'Marelle, 'The people of Waterford will always be grateful. We wish you a safe onward journey.'

Accepting the outlaw's handshake, D'Marelle gave a half bow. 'It has been interesting meeting you, Robin Hood.'

'Likewise.' Turning to his friends, Robin made ready to take his leave. 'Okay everyone, let's get Alwin back to Dora or she'll worry when the villagers arrive without him.'

They were only one step from the safety of the

trees when a commanding shout rang out behind them, and the convivial atmosphere dissolved.

'*Now!*'

As one, the outlaws spun around. The whole forest seemed to groan as they were met with the sight of D'Marelle's men drawing their swords.

In less than a second, the encounter between the soldiers and the outlaws had changed from an amiable prisoner exchange to a deadly challenge.

Robin's roar of disappointment morphed into pure anger as D'Marelle's men attacked. Drawing Albion, his sword, Robin launched himself at the king's man. 'D'Marelle!'

Scarlett's sword clashed fast and hard with the nearest assailant. With each strike he shouted out years of hatred. 'I knew it! Once a weasel—'

The scrape of Will's sword was accompanied by the fast-moving hollow thud of Little John's quarterstaff as it found its mark again and again. A moment later, a soldier's enthusiastic onslaught was cut short as he was knocked cold by the force of John's skilled strokes.

As the fight accelerated, D'Marelle shouted, 'Take them all. Even the woman and the fat friar can swell the king's numbers in France.'

The recruiter's casual dismissal of Marion and

Tuck lent power to Robin's sword arm. 'Scarlet was right about you.'

D'Marelle's arms may have been old, but they remained strong, and with each strike of his sword he pushed Robin nearer the waiting wagons. 'King John's war needs fighting, and it needs men to fight it. The more recruits I have, the better.'

Battling harder, Robin surged forwards, edging his opponent nearer Sherwood. 'You fight well for an old man.'

D'Marelle laughed with short, rasping gasps. 'Give up. Robin. There's no point in risking your men being damaged before they get to the ships.'

'You really would send Marion, wouldn't you?'

Missing slicing Robin's cheek by the tiniest margin, D'Marelle swung his sword again, its blade meeting Albion with a heavy thud. 'I can't see anyone crying over an outlaw's woman.'

Looking past D'Marelle, Robin saw that the skirmish had become a determined battle. The outlaws were trying to force the soldiers towards Sherwood, while the recruiter's men were desperate to stay in the relative safety of the open road.

Gravel, stray twigs, and leaves crunched under boots and anxious hooves alike. Each time the outlaws overcame a guard, another seemed to appear, ready to take their place. Robin Hood's followers were fighting a never-ending battle.

His sword arm heavy from the nonstop onslaught, Scarlet's rage kept him going. He could see Much's strained exertion as he struggled to block his enemy's weapon, and knew his friend was tiring. Even Marion's well-aimed arrows were making little dent in the number of guards.

More cross with himself than with D'Marelle, Will spat out his words. 'I knew it! Didn't I say there'd be treachery? I should have seen there were too many soldiers guarding so few prisoners. Stupid… Stupid… Ahhh…'

Guards wearing the livery of King John suddenly ran into the fray, and Robin saw what Scarlet had already worked out. D'Marelle had hidden an extra force of men in the trees. Cursing, he fought on. The only chance they had now was for him to overcome D'Marelle himself, and fast.

A loud smack resounded through the melee as the flat of a sword met the side of Will's head, knocking him to the ground. No sooner had his knees hit the floor, when two pairs of mail gloved hands dug into his shoulders. Ignoring his protests, the men dragged him, kicking and yelling, into the nearest cart. 'Let me go! Let me goooo…'

Scarlet's voice was muffled as, landing a last punch on one of his captors, he was thrown bodily into the waiting cart, the doors bolted fast behind him.

Much, slipping through the hands of his current attacker thanks to an arrow from Marion's bow, ran to Robin—each footstep echoed by the sound of Scarlet's fists thumping against the inside of the cart. Arriving as near to Robin as it was safe to get, Much shouted, 'Will's been caught. Robin, he's... OUCH!'

A soldier had emerged from the trees at speed, knocking Much to the ground with a single punch to the side of his head, before disappearing into the heart of the fight, his sword at the ready.

Much's slumped form landed at Little John's feet. Seeing his friend's fallen body, the giant gave a roar of distress, the sound of wood against metal filling his ears as he fought with a renewed desperation to end the fight before any of the other outlaws were hurt.

Directing the rain of his strokes so that he forced his opponent nearer Robin, John called out, 'Much is being taken to the cart... Hold on—'

The whirl of wood whistled as the staff arched through the air and, as John's weapon found its target, another sickening thud filled the crossroads. It was the unmistakeable sound of a heavy blow to the stomach followed by a familiar cry.

Tuck dropped to his knees, clutching his belly, 'Robin—'

Her arrows spent, Marion's sword clashed as she fought back-to-back with Nasir. The double swipe of the Saracen's swords abruptly ceasing, as a screech accompanied the fall of a soldier, a deep blade wound to his chest.

'One less to worry about.'

Cowering at the roadside, huddled far from where D'Marelle's reinforcements had been hidden, Alwin watched, his eyes wide with terror.

'This is wrong. All wrong.' Managing to tear his gaze from the cart where Much and Will had been stowed, Alwin tried to work out what to do.

'I must help them. But how?' Trying not to let panic overtake him, he closed his eyes to help him think. 'I'll do my ritual. It will keep them safe.'

Opening his eyes again, keeping them trained on the fight ahead, Alwin searched his fingers though the dirt until they closed around a twig. Talking himself into a state of normality, he said, 'Next, I climb.'

Frightened, but feeling better now he was doing something, Alwin sat on a thick branch, his legs swinging, tapping the short stick against the trunk as if he was sat in his tree at home.

'Herne. Can you hear me?' Alwin spoke fast, the urgency of the drama unfolding before him lending wings to his words as he fell into his chant, 'Mighty forest, I beseech thee, through the power of this ritual, and the strength of Herne, Lord of the Trees, to protect my mother, myself and all who live under the shadow of Sherwood.'

As Little John toppled the soldier he was fighting to the ground, Alwin banged the twig harder against the trunk, his chant morphing into a shout of defiance. 'Robin is in trouble. Herne! Can't you hear me? Your son needs help. Sherwood needs them more than France does. Protect them.'

He could see that the remaining outlaws were tiring, and Alwin knew if their fatigue was obvious to him, then D'Marelle would have noticed too, and already be tasting victory. Mouthing out his words, Alwin beseeched his new friends, 'Robin! Fight harder. Don't give up. *Please* don't give up. Much has to be freed. He's my friend.'

The roadside had become a brawl of dead or unconscious soldiers and clanging metal. Only one man-at-arms per outlaw remained now, but still D'Marelle gloated. 'You're not such a good fighter as I'd been led to believe Robin Hood.'

Robin's reply was lost as Alwin let out a piercing scream. 'Herne! Robin's in trouble!'

Although John's expression told Alwin he'd been heard, there was no way the big man could help anyone but himself as he continued to fight.

A cold realisation stole over Alwin. It was all down to him. Robin and Much had saved him, now he had to save them.

Lowering himself to the ground, mindful of all Much's warnings about watching where he trod, Alwin made his way to Robin, keeping to the side of the road, staying as sheltered as he could until the last minute.

After hesitating undercover for a second, Alwin sprinted into the fray. 'Robin, Robin!'

Taken by surprised by the new arrival, D'Marelle's sword missed its mark for the first time.

'Who the hell..?' Shoving the boy out of the way in his attempt to avoid stabbing him rather than Robin, the recruiter's sword slipped again, the squeal of metal grating on his already tightly strung nerves.

'Richard?' Temporarily unable to co-ordinate, D'Marelle's expression was a confusion of sorrow and frustration, 'For a moment, I thought...'

The distraction was all Robin needed. Rushing at the recruiter, he pushed him backwards and drew his knife. Robin had a blade at D'Marelle's throat and a foot on his chest before his enemy's back had thudded against the road's hard surface. 'I'd stay *exactly* where you are if I was you, my Lord.'

The final few strikes of metal and wood behind them faulted, before fading to a halt as the soldiers saw that their master had been overpowered.

Robin pushed his knife closer to the recruiter's loose-skinned neck. 'Tell them to drop their weapons.'

With a voice laced more with wonder than defeat, D'Marelle commanded, 'Do as he says.'

A reluctant metallic clatter followed, as the swords of the remaining soldiers hit the ground.

Issuing out swift instructions, Robin sent John and Nasir to free Scarlet and Much, before reaching his free hand out to Marion. 'Are you alright?'

Brushing some dust from Robin's cheek, Marion nodded, 'Just bruised. You?'

'I'm fine. Could you check on Tuck?'

'Of course.' Marion headed to the fallen cleric, whose legs were beginning to stir as he emerged from his stunned state.

Having ensured his followers were alright, his foot lodged against D'Marelle's torso, Robin beckoned to the boy from Waterford. 'Thank you, Alwin.'

'It wasn't me, it was my ritual.' Alwin waved a hand at the forest. 'I asked the trees for help. I asked Herne. My prayer worked, didn't it.'

Robin inclined his head. 'It did. You were very brave.'

D'Marelle, not bothering to try and move from his position on the dusty hinterland between the roadside and the forest, asked, 'Who is this boy?'

Confident that his ritual had worked just as he'd always said it would, Alwin stepped forward. 'I'm Alwin, my Lord. Are you alright?'

'What?' D'Marelle grappled to comprehend the concern the young man was showing for his welfare. 'I was just fighting your friend. Why are you asking if I'm alright?'

'Cos you look hot and tired.'

His eyebrows rising, D'Marelle conceded, 'I'm a bit old for this, that's all…' Then, as if remembering himself, D'Marelle switched his attention back to Robin. 'You only beat me because of a boy, Wolfshead! Hardly a tale to add to the legend!'

Robin kept his voice steady. 'A boy who you were going to take to France to die.'

D'Marelle's throat went dry as he stuttered, 'I had to…'

Shaking his head, Robin bent to the fallen man. 'You were prepared to do to Alwin what you did to your son. Something you claim you regretted.'

Protesting now, D'Marelle said, 'But this was the only way to—'

Interrupting again, Alwin knelt next to the knight. 'Are you sure you are alright, my Lord? Here…' He wiped the older man's brow with a handful of leaves. 'If I use these, then I can clean your forehead of sweat. There… is that better?'

Speechless, D'Marelle could only stare at the lad as Robin repeated, 'You were going to send this boy into a war. You should be ashamed!'

'I am.' Keeping his stunned gaze on the boy, D'Marelle asked, 'May I sit up?'

With an incline of Robin's head, D'Marelle sat slowly, brushing the dirt from his hands as he did so. Acting as if Robin's knife, which remained at his throat, was not there, the recruiter spoke to Alwin. 'Thank you. You are so like him. My son, Richard. He talked to trees too. He was about the same age when I last saw him.'

Not risking being taken in by D'Marelle a second time, Robin dragged the recruiter to his feet by the tunic, just as the sound of an angry bull of a shout was heard revving up in the background. 'You broke your word. Explain yourself or I'll let Scarlet demonstrate just how outraged he can get.'

Will had jumped from the cart and was now hurtling towards Robin and D'Marelle at full pelt. 'You utter—'

'Oh dear, too late.' Half-smiled Robin.

Knocking D'Marelle back to the ground with the force of the slap that he launched at the older man's face, Scarlet leapt on top of his quarry. 'I ought to kill you right now, you filthy piece of scum.' Will slapped the soldier's face repeatedly with the flat of his palms. Robin was happy to let him vent his frustration right up until Scarlet picked a fallen knife from the ground.

'Enough!' Robin's voice rang clear. 'For once I find myself in agreement with King John. This man doesn't deserve such an easy death.'

CHAPTER FOURTEEN

Handing a simmering Scarlet into the care of Tuck
and Nasir, Robin gave his knife to Marion so she
could guard D'Marelle, while he, Little John and
Much dragged the fallen soldiers off the road.
Hiding the casualties under the cover of the forest,
they locked the remainder of D'Marelle's men in the
carts along with the jeering prisoners.

Only when the crossroads no longer resembled
a battlefield did Robin lead the outlaws and their
prisoner into the safety of Sherwood. Once they
were deep within the forest, Robin pushed the
recruiter to the ground and, standing over him, his
arms folded, Robin barked, 'Explain yourself.'

'I'm truly sorry.'

Scarlet, in no mood to accept an apology, was

only prevented from knocking the living daylights out of D'Marelle by Little John's restraining arm. He snarled, 'Too late for sorry. *Way* too late.'

'Nevertheless, I am.'

Passing Robin's knife back to him, Marion said, 'Tell us. Help us understand.'

As she waited for an answer, Marion joined Alwin, who had sat himself down, cross-legged, before D'Marelle. It wasn't until the boy nodded his encouragement that the recruiter began to speak.

'It's simple, really. I thought if I captured you. *All* of you. If I took Robin Hood, his men, and you Lady Marion, to France, King John might release me from my duties.'

Robin, his knife to hand, spoke bluntly. 'You thought you'd swap us for your role as chief recruiter.'

'I'm tired of sending men to die.'

Despite the ring of shame to D'Marelle's voice, Scarlet was unmoved. 'Took you long enough to get tired of it!'

D'Marelle levelled his eyes on Will. 'It's time I went back. Time I went to France with the new soldiers. I need to face what I have done before it's too late.'

'I think I understand.' Marion picked a stone from the floor, rolling it in her hands as she said,

'You're ready to say goodbye to your son? To beg his forgiveness in the land where he died.'

'I've never even had the chance to visit Richard's grave. It's time I tried to put at least that error right.'

D'Marelle was quiet for moment before he switched his gaze from Marion to the boy sat next to her. 'You were very brave. What did you say your name was again?'

'Alwin, my Lord.'

'I'd like to thank you, Alwin. You stopped me doing something else I'd regret. You should be proud of yourself.'

Alwin looked at Herne's Son, his small round face determined. 'We have to let him go to say goodbye to Richard, Robin.'

'Is that's what you want, Alwin?'

'Yes. It's the right thing to do.'

Robin, his face devoid of emotion, addressed D'Marelle. 'Take your men and go. And *don't* return. Not to Sherwood and not to England. Not ever.'

D'Marelle clambered to his feet. He was heading to the carts to see how many of his guards were conscious enough to ride when Scarlet's angry protest exploded from his lips. 'You can't just let him go! He'd have had us all killed in battle if he'd got his way. Even Marion!'

'But he didn't.'

'Robin! He...' Will shook with anger. 'You didn't see. You don't know!'

Placing a hand on his friend's shoulder, Robin nodded. 'I didn't see, and I'll never truly know what hell you've been through, Will. I am just thankful that you survived them and came to us. To Sherwood, so you could help us. And helping us sometimes means giving people that have made a mistake a second chance. Yes?'

'Some people yes. Others don't deserve one.'

Not moving from their sheltered position beneath the trees, Alwin and the outlaws watched as the impatient horses were circled round to face in the direction of Lincoln.

Calling from his mount, D'Marelle said, 'Thank you, Robin Hood.'

'Don't thank me. Thank, Alwin.'

D'Marelle studied the boy. The lad's face had a new serenity about it now the danger had passed. 'Thank you, Alwin of Waterford.'

As the recruiter nudged his horse into a steady

trot, Robin called out, 'Don't let your son down a third time.'

The rumble of the horses and carts had faded into the distance before Will spoke, his words laced with bitterness. 'Is that it then? All those deaths on his hands and we just let him go?'

Walking on one side of Scarlet, while Robin kept pace on the other, Marion said, 'Whatever he does next, Will, he'll be in France doing it. He won't be here.'

'I suppose so.'

Hanging back to let Marion make her way along a thin path before them, Robin said, 'And don't forget, Will. He's going to Normandy without King John's permission. He's supposed to stay here and keep recruiting. In France, James D'Marelle will always be looking over his shoulder. Not only because he'll be alongside all those men he condemned to battle on foreign shores. But he'll always be wondering what the punishment for his disobedience towards King John will be, and when it will arrive.'

Rubbing at his face, the bruise left by the guard's

sword already a mottled green and purple, Will mumbled, 'It's bad enough to lose a wife, but to lose a son…' His voice faded, as he was consumed by the memories he'd buried for so long that it hurt even to consider their existence.

After he'd been quiet for a while, as they continued to weave their way towards Waterford, Marion asked, 'Are you alright, Will?'

'He, D'Marelle, he didn't force me to go to France, Marion. The others, the men I fought with, he forced them. But me… I went willingly. I was glad to go. To escape the memories of—'

'Oh, Will.' Marion put an arm around her friend, knowing that memories of Elena, his sorely missed wife, were assaulting him from the inside; the pain of the bruising on his battered face would be nothing by comparison.

'Come on, let's get Alwin back to his mother.'

'And then go home?'

'And then go home.'

Also from Chinbeard and Oak Tree Books...

Richard Carpenter's
ROBIN OF SHERWOOD

MATHILDA'S LEGACY

Jennifer Ash

You may also enjoy…